JAMES JONES

is one of the truly great novelists of our time—a storyteller whose power and grip on the reader is as irresistible as it is unforgettable.

THE PISTOL

ranks as one of the greatest triumphs of the author of such mighty works as **From Here to Eternity** and **Whistle**. Here is a drama of one lone man against the world. Here is an epic of raw, stubborn human courage and indomitable will to survive.

"It has the drive of a punch to the solar plexus!"
—Detroit News

BY JAMES JONES

The Pistol

James Jones

A Dell Book

Published by
DELL PUBLISHING CO., INC.
1 Dag Hammarskjold Plaza
New York, New York 10017

Dell ® TM 681510, Dell Publishing Co., Inc.

ISBN: 0-440-17068-0

Reprinted by arrangement with
Charles Scribner's Sons
New York, New York

Printed in the United States of America
Previous Dell Edition #7068
New Dell Edition
First printing—April 1979

This book is not dedicated to anything or anybody. I would dedicate it to my wife Gloria, who helped as wife and as reader, were it not that I am tired of books dedicated to wives by men who are grateful to their wives for being wives. My wife agrees with me.

The Pistol

CHAPTER ONE

When the first bombs lit at Wheeler Field on December 7, 1941, Pfc Richard Mast was eating breakfast. He was also wearing a pistol. From where Mast sat, amidst the bent heads, quiet murmur, and soft, cutlery-against-china sounds of breakfast, in a small company mess in one of the infantry quadrangles of Schofield Barracks, it was perhaps a mile to Wheeler Field, and it took several seconds for the sound of the explosions, followed soon after by the shockwave through the earth, to reach his ears. Obviously, as far as Mast was concerned during those few seconds, the United States was still at peace, although in actual fact she was already, even then, at war. Consequently, during those moments, Mast had no idea at all of getting to keep the pistol he was wearing.

In one way it was unusual for a soldier in

peacetime to be wearing a pistol at breakfast, but in another way it was not. The day before, on Saturday's duty roster, Mast and three other men had been named to go on Interior Guard duty. This guard duty lasted from four in the afternoon to four in the afternoon, twenty-four hours, and the men assigned to it daily from the various companies drew pistols, pistol belts, arm brassards and pistol lanyards from their company supply rooms. They were required to sign for these, required to wear them at all times when they were not actually sleeping, and twenty-four hours later when they came off guard, required to turn them back immediately. This was a strict rule. No exceptions to it were allowed in any form. There was a good reason for it.

In our Army, back in those now-dead, very far-off times, pistols were at a premium. The regulation .45-caliber automatic pistol adopted by the Army was a beautiful thing; it was also a potent weapon at close range. But perhaps even more important, it was small enough to steal. It would be pretty hard for any soldier who was being discharged to steal a rifle, even if he dismantled it completely. Not so with the pistol, and any man would have dearly loved to get his hands on a loose one, without signed records following it around. This, however, was next to impossible to do. Not only was very careful track kept of them, but they were also very scarce in an infantry regiment, since they were issued only to Headquarters personnel, officers, and members of machinegun squads. As a result, about the only time a straight duty rifle private like Mast ever got to put his hands on one, was the twenty-four hours when he went on guard.

All this, of course, went into Mast's enjoyment of wearing, handling and possessing, for twenty-four hours at least, a pistol. But for Mast, who was nineteen and imaginative, there was an even greater pleasure in it. Wearing a pistol on his hip made him feel more like a real soldier, seemed to give him an unbroken lineal connection with the Army of the days of the West and Custer's Cavalry, made him feel that he was really in the Army, a feeling Mast did not often have in what to himself he termed this crumby, lazy outfit. It was almost enough to offset his irritation at having his weekend pass spoiled by guard duty on Sunday.

After the first rack of bombs went off and the sound and shockwave reached the little company mess, there was almost a full minute of thoughtful silence during which everyone looked at everyone else. "Dynamiting?" somebody said. Then another rack fell and exploded and at the same time the first plane came screeching over the quadrangle, its machine guns going full blast. After that there wasn't any doubt and the entire mess jumped up to rush outside.

Mast, being careful to catch up his Sunday half pint of milk so no one could steal it, went too, his pistol riding reassuringly on his hip. A pistol obviously wasn't much good against strafing airplanes, but just the same it felt good to him to have it. It gave Mast a sort of swaggery confidence. He wished rather wistfully, as he watched the next plane come over, that he did not have to turn it in tonight when he went off guard.

It was pretty exciting outside the quadrangle in the street. Out here you could see a big column of black smoke beginning to rise up through the bright morning air from down at Wheeler Field where they were bombing the planes. You could see them twinkling up there in the sun. They looked innocent, as though they had nothing to do with the destruction going on below.

Every few minutes a fighter with the red discs painted on the wings and fuselage would come screeching and blasting over, his MG fire raking the street. Then everyone would surge back against the building. As soon as he was gone, they would surge right back out again and stand staring at the smoke column as if they were personally responsible for it and proud of their achievement. They looked as though they wanted to take credit for the whole thing themselves, without giving the Japs any at all.

Mast, surging backward and forward with them, had an excited feeling of being in on history, of actually seeing history made, and he wondered if any of the other men felt that way. But Mast doubted if they did. Most of them weren't too bright, or very educated.

Mast happened to be one of three high school graduates in his company, and this fact often worked against him, in many ways. Of the other two, one was company clerk and a sergeant, and the other had been carried off on special duty to work in battalion intelligence and was a tech sergeant. But Mast had steadfastly refused to be inveigled into any such job. If he had wanted to be a clerk, he could have enlisted in the Air Corps. As a result, Mast was the only high school graduate doing straight duty as a rifle private in his company, and in a company like this, where almost nobody had completed grade school, almost no one liked or trusted a man who had finished high school.

For a moment, excitedly, Mast thought of drawing his pistol and taking a few blasts at the low-flying planes as they came over, but he was afraid of looking absurd or ridiculous so he didn't. Even though he had made Expert in pistol on the range, he was reasonably sure he would never hit one. But, boy! Mast thought, what if he did hit one? did bring one down single-handed all by himself with his pistol? What a hero he would be, and at only nineteen! Hell, maybe he'd even get a medal. He could imagine the whole thing in his mind as he allowed himself to be jostled back by the men in front as another plane screamed over: the general, the regimental band playing the parade on the division parade ground, the whole business. Boy, what would they think about *that* back home in Miseryville? Even so, he was still too embarrassed, too afraid of being laughed at, to haul the pistol out.

Actually, Mast was the only man present with

a weapon, since the other three men on guard with him had to stay over at the guardhouse and sleep there. That was where Mast himself would have been, if he had not been picked an orderly at guardmount yesterday. Wishing he dared draw it, Mast let his hand fall down to his side and massaged the holster flap of his pistol he knew he would have to turn back this evening.

Just then a heavy hand was laid on his shoulder. Startled, Mast turned around to see First Sergeant Wycoff, a big man in his thirties, looking at him with angry eyes and the same numb, stupid, half-grinning expression on his face that all the others had, including his own.

"Mast, aren't you on guard orderly today?"

"What? Oh. Yeah. Yeah, I am."

"Then you better get your tail on over to Headquarters and report," the First Sergeant said, not unkindly. "They'll probably be needing you for carrying messages."

"Okay," Mast said; "yes, sir," and began to shoulder his way back inside through the press, finishing his bottle of milk as he went. Now why the hell hadn't he thought of that himself? he wondered.

Inside the quadrangle, after he had gone back through the building, Mast found men were running everywhere. Whenever a plane came roaring, sliding over they broke and scattered like bowling pins. Then they would get back up and go back to their running. Mast saw one man actually get shot in the leg. It was unbelievable.

He simply fell down and lay there with his head up beating his fists on the ground, whether in anger or anguish Mast could not tell. After the planes passed he was helped to the side lines by two men who ran out, dragging his leg for all the world like an injured football player being helped out of the game.

Up on the roofs of the quadrangle men had begun to appear with machine guns and BARs and were now firing back at the planes as they came over, and from his vantage point under the porch Mast watched them, envying them hungrily. Of all days, he would have to be on guard today; and not only that, would have to get himself picked as guard orderly.

Mast had been on guard plenty of times in the past, but he had never before been chosen orderly. This was because he always became nervous when it came to answering the General Orders questions. He always looked as polished at inspection as everyone else, and he had the General Orders memorized. But whenever the Officer of the Day asked him the questions he would freeze, and his mind would go blank.

And now today of all days, Mast thought regretfully, he would have to make it for orderly. Usually it was the most coveted job, because all you had to do was sit around Headquarters all day outside the Colonel's office and you got your whole night off to yourself, while the rest of them had to stand two hours on and four off, around the clock.

Well, that was just about what he might have expected, Mast thought sadly, have figured on, his customary luck: guard orderly on the day the dirty Japs attacked Oahu.

Standing in under the covered porch and watching the scene before him, a sad, bitter melancholy crept over Mast. It was a feeling that even the longest life was short and the end of it was death and extinction and then rotting away, and that about all a man could expect along the way was frustration, and bitterness, and phoniness in everybody, and hatred. Perhaps being a high school graduate in a company of oafs contributed to it a little bit.

Disdaining to run like the rest of them, even though he could not help feeling a certain nervousness, Mast composed his face into a contemptuous smirk and came out from under the protection of the porch and walked slowly around the square, his pistol swaying bravely on his hip. Twice as he walked flame-spitting planes came sliding over, churning up twin rows of dust across the grass and richocheting screamingly off the brick, and Mast could feel the muscles of his back twitch, but he refused to let himself run or even walk faster.

From under one of the porches of the 3rd Battalion an officer yelled at him, angrily, indignantly, outraged: "Hey, you silly son of a bitch! Get out of there! Are you crazy? Move! Run! That's an order!"

Mast turned his head to look at him, but he did

not stop or change his gait. Then suddenly emotion spurted out of him like blood gushing out of a wound. "Go to hell" he shouted happily, knowing that for once he was invulnerable even to an officer. Just then a third plane came screeching, blasting over and his eyes began to blink themselves rapidly, as if that act in itself would offer him protection. Then it was gone, just like that, off over the quad. In some odd way of possessive ownership, of just knowing it was there, the pistol on his hip helped shore up Mast's courage. He sure wished he didn't have to turn it in tonight. It wasn't like a rifle. Didn't give you the same feeling at all. What the damned government *ought* to do was issue every trooper a rifle and pistol both. They used to. In the Cavalry.

In the Headquarters building upstairs outside the Colonel's office, when Mast got there, everything was in an uproar. Officers were running all over the place, bumping into each other, getting in each other's way. They all had the same numb, stupid, excited look the men in Mast's company had had, the same look Mast could feel on his own face, and once again Mast was struck with that awareness that he was actually *seeing* history made.

When he finally saw the Adjutant coming out of the Old Man's office, he reported to him and told him he was here.

"What? Oh," the middle-aged first lieutenant said, looking numbly excited, as well as harassed. "Well, stick around. May have something for you to do. Messages or something." He hurried off. Mast sat back down. What a way to spend the bombing of Hawaii. Outside the Jap fighters continued to scream over the quad, blasting. Inside, high-ranking officers continued to bump into each other in their hurry. And Mast sat.

It was some time after the attack was over, several hours, before the adjutant found time to release Mast and send him back to his company. They would not need him further. In the interim he had been sent out with a series of messages from the colonel to the various battalion and company commanders about moving out, and twice he was sent by the adjutant to the motor pool to find out what was holding the trucks up, but that was all.

Slowly Mast trudged back across the quad that was now swarming with activity. Not only had he missed almost all of the attack, but this release of the guard to take the field meant that he would have to turn in the pistol, and all Mast could think of was that if the Japs were landing (or *had* landed), what a wonderful personal defense weapon that pistol would be. Especially against those Samurai sabers of the officers, about which he had read so much. Because as soon as the other three men on guard reported back also, they would all be required to turn in their pistols for which they'd signed. Gloomily he kicked at a clod ahead of him that a Jap MG had churned up from the green.

When he got back to the company area the first

thing Mast found out, however, from one of the disgruntled privates who had been detailed to help load the kitchen truck, was that the other three men from the company were staying behind. The entire Interior Regimental Guard with the sole exception of the orderly, which was himself of course, had been ordered to stay behind and continue their guarding duties until some provision for relieving them could be organized.

For a moment, as he heard this, Mast thought of just going on upstairs and hiding the pistol away in his full-field pack. It would certainly go unnoticed, perhaps for a long time, in this confusion. Perhaps forever. That was what he wanted to do. But what good would the pistol do him if the Japs were on the beaches and it was in his pack? Anyway, he thought with defeat, he had signed his name for it. And some essential of Mast's childhood training, some inherent nervousness at the idea of going against authority, some guilt, and the shame of getting caught, refused to let him do what he desired. Now, if he hadn't signed his name—Hell, it wasn't even simple honestly, Mast raged at himself, it was just plain fear.

But he still couldn't make himself do it. So instead he temporized. Still wearing the pistol and the other accounterments of guard duty, he went into the Orderly Room to report to the first sergeant, to see what might happen. Maybe the First wouldn't even notice it.

"What? Oh," First Sergeant Wycoff said, looking up with harassed eyes. He was behind his desk packing files and report books. "Released you? Well, turn in your gear and go upstairs and pack, Mast," he said, not unkindly. "Field uniform, full-field pack, one barracks bag."

"Yes, sir." Mast's spirits fell. He turned to go.

"And Mast," First Sergeant Wycoff said sharply.

Mast turned around, his heart in his mouth from guilt. He was caught. "Sir?"

"Don't worry about time," the First Sergeant said bitterly, without even looking up. "There'll be plenty of goddamned time for you to pack." He slammed his Morning Report book into a musette bag.

"Yes, sir."

Outside, Mast tried to analyze it. The First had told him to turn in his gear. Okay. That was obviously more or less an order. On the other hand, Wycoff had not mentioned the pistol specifically or even looked at it. But then perhaps that was because he always wore one himself when the company was in the field. In addition to his rifle, Mast remembered bitterly. Well, he couldn't very well turn in the other stuff without the pistol. Reluctantly, loving the feel of the pistol on him and in his hand more now than ever before—especially when he thought about those Samurai sabers, Mast turned toward the supply room.

He was saved by the supply clerk. This soldier, a long, thin stringbean of an Italian Pfc who had been in the Army at least twelve years, was now in charge of another disgruntled detail drafted at random to load the supply truck, sitting in the street behind the kitchen truck. He only snarled.

"For God's sake, Mast! Don't bother me with a lousy pistol and brassard," he screamed, shaking at Mast a .30-caliber watercooled he was carrying. "I got im*port*ant things to do. Them goddam beaches are probably crawling with Jap infantry right now."

"Okay, I'm sorry," Mast said, and carefully veiled his surprised happiness under a look of hurt vanity.

Morally exonerated now, and relieved, although not without a certain nervousness at the thought of those beaches crawling with Jap infantry (crawling: like ants: all over you), he went upstairs to pack. The pistol still rode his hip heavily, a weight pregnant with compressed power, symbolic of an obscure personal safety. No wonder everybody wanted pistols. And he himself could not be held accountable for thievery: he had tried to give it back.

CHAPTER TWO

The second floor squadroom was alive with movement of men kneeling and straining at packstraps, men stooping to stuff barracks bags with extra clothes. Moving out! As he rolled his own pack, Mast thought once again about packing the pistol away so no one would see it. If he did, maybe nobody would *ever* remember it. But if the Japs *were* on the beaches, already, he would want it immediately. And if the company dropped their packs going into action as they surely would, and the pistol was in his pack— . . .

Well aware that he was taking a real chance of eventually losing it back to the supply room, Mast decided to gamble and wear it anyway. What good would it do him, what protection, lying in a barracks bag or pack? Luckily it was a regulation holster and not the kind the MPs wore. All he had to do was unhook it off the web pistol belt, hook it into his rifle cartridge belt, and stuff the extra clips into the cartridge pockets above it. The brassard and lanyard he packed in the bottom of the barracks bag with the pistol belt. Then, wearing his tin hat with a jauntiness he did not entirely feel when he thought about what might be in store for them, Mast carted everything downstairs to the yard where the company was slowly forming. Sergeant Wycoff had certainly been right about the time. There was another full hour and a half to wait, and it was nearly three o'clock before the personnel trucks of the Regiment began to move.

On the way down to the beaches in the trucks Mast received only one comment on the pistol. A Private 1st Class in the same truck but from another platoon, a huge blue-jowled black Irishman of twenty-two named O'Brien, asked him enviously where did he get the pistol?

"That?" Mast said coolly, but with his mind working swiftly. "Oh, I've had that a long time. Bought it off a guy."

O'Brien moved his big dark face inarticulately, wrinkling his broad forehead and moistening his lips, then flexed his hamlike hands a couple of times where they dangled from his knees. He stared at the holstered pistol hungrily, almost abjectly. Then he turned his huge dark head with the pale green eyes and stared off levelly from the back of the open truck with its hastily mounted MG on the cab roof, toward where the sea was.

Mast had seen him engaged in some tremendous, almost Herculean fist fights since he had been in the company, but he did not look tough now. He turned back to Mast. "Want to sell it?" he said huskily.

"Sell it? Hell, no. That's why I bought it."

O'Brien reached one big-fingered hand up and unbuttoned his shirt pocket and pulled out a wad of bills. "Made some money on craps last night," he said almost wistfully. "Give you fifty bucks for it."

Mast was astonished, and did not think he had heard right. He had had no idea his new possession would be so valuable—not to anyone but himself. But there was O'Brien, and there was the money. Nobody else in the truck was paying any attention.

"No," Mast said. "Nosir. I want it for myself."

"Give you seventy," O'Brien said quietly, almost beseechingly. "That's all I got."

"No dice. I told you. That's why I bought it in the first place. So I could have it for myself."

"Well, hell," O'Brien said hopelessly, and slowly put his useless money back in the pocket and buttoned the flap. Unhappily he clutched his rifle, and out of the broad, dark, brooding face with its pale green eyes stared off in the direction of the sea again.

But that was the only comment. No one else noticed the pistol apparently, not even Mast's own squad leader. They were all too concerned with thinking about what they might find on the beaches. Mast could not help feeling rather smugly sorry for O'Brien, somewhat the same feeling a man who knows he has salvation experiences for one who knows he has not; but Mast did not know what he could be expected to do. There was only one pistol. And through fate, or luck, and a series of strangely unforeseeable happenings, it had been given to him, not O'Brien.

Mast and O'Brien were not the only ones who kept looking off toward where the sea was. If the colonel knew that the Japanese forces had not landed, he might possibly have told the Company Commander. But if he had, the Company Commander had not seen fit to tell his troops. Perhaps the truth was that nobody knew. At any rate, the men in the truck did not. And as the convoy, moving by fits and starts, wound its way down off the high central plateau of the island, there were places between the hills where the men could get clear glimpses far away below them of the smoking shambles of Pearl Harbor and Hickam Field. The sight made them even more thoughtful. As far away as they could see, a mile-long line of trucks was worming its way down bumper to bumper, carrying them at a pace a man could walk, toward Honolulu and they knew not what else.

Actually, long before they ever reached the city everybody knew the Japanese had not landed. The word was shouted back from truck to truck, traveling far faster than the trucks themselves went forward. But the knowledge reassured nobody. If they didn't land today, they would tomorrow, or the next day. And going through the city there was very little friendly response by the men in the trucks to the wildly cheering civilians who only so recently as last night had wanted nothing to do with soldiers except take their money.

The method in which the trucks had been loaded back at Schofield by Regimental Order was planned in advance so that the men and equipment for each beach position would be loaded all on the same truck, or trucks. Consequently, the little section of the miles-long convoy which was Mast's company (whose sector ran from Wailupe east through Koko Head to Makapuu Head), having split off from the main trunk highway and made its way through the city on back roads, found itself alone out on Kamehameha Highway going east, its trucks peeling off one by one from the head of the column as it came abreast of their positions, until finally only four were left: the four trucks for the Company's last and biggest position at Makapuu Point, one of which trucks was Mast's. The effect was weird, if not downright enervating: From a huge, powerful convoy of unnumbered men and vehicles they had dwindled down to just four trucks, alone, moving along a deserted highway between the mountains and the sea and filled with thirty-five puny men and eighteen puny machine guns, all that was left, apparently, to fight the war alone against the entire might of the Imperial Japanese war machine. Or so they felt. Mast could not help feeling a shiver, in spite of his pleasure over his new pistol.

Makapuu Head, and Point, was acknowledgedly the worst position in the company sector. For one thing, there were no civilian homes within miles, such as the majority of the company's position had, and hence no civilians by whom to be admired, and from whom to bum food. For another, it was at the very extreme end of the company chow line and by the time the little weapons carriers that brought the food got to them, the food itself in the big aluminum pots was so cold the grease would be congealed on top of it. For a third, Makapoo (as they came at once to call it) was the only position in the company sector large enough to have a truly autonomous military organization; most of the positions had four, or five, or even seven, men and were run by a single sergeant or corporal; not Makapoo: it had thirty-five, its own private lieutenant, six sergeants, and at least four corporals. And, as every soldier knows, a sergeant who has an officer observing him does not act at all the same as a sergeant who is on his own.

For a fourth thing, Makapuu Point was the very hub and apex of what the Islanders preferred to call the 'Windward' side of Oahu. Jutting far out into the sea all by itself, there was nothing between it and San Francisco, and the wind that poured against the Pali and shot straight up, strongly enough to keep more than one would-be suicide from obtaining more than a couple of broken legs by a fall of more than a hundred feet, poured across it also, a living river of air, a tidal ocean of it. 'Windward' was a pretty lax term for such a wind, if you had to live in it without relief. And at Makapoo you were never free of it. It never ceased. Even in the pillboxes cut into the living rock in November, the wind seeped in like water and made chilling eddies of air among the shivering men who tried to sleep there.

And if these were not enough to earn Makapoo its title of 'A-hole of the Universe,' for a fifth thing, there was not a single building there to take shelter in; nor was there enough loose dirt on top the solid rock to drive a tentpeg into. This was the beach position Richard Mast, with his customary luck, had managed to get himself assigned to; and this was the beach position they scrambled out of the trucks that first day to try and make, first, militarily defensible, and then second, livable.

The first week of both of these attempts was hectic, what with the Japanese expected every day, and also ridiculous. It consisted mainly (after having first got the MGs set up in their proper fields of fire in the pillboxes) of putting up all day barbed wire which far more often than not the sea washed away, of standing guard half the night, and of having one's shelterhalf and two blankets blown off of one during the rest of the night by the wind. There was consequently very little sleep. No matter how tightly and carefully a man might wrap up, the wind, testing here, trying there, eventually would find a loose corner somewhere with which to begin its endless and seemingly diabolical tug of war. There was not room enough for most of the men to sleep 'indoors,' if the rock floors of the pillboxes could be called that, and most of them had to lie down outside on the stony ground in the full force of the wind. No one had thought to try to provide sleeping shelter for the men.

But even all of this discomfort, together with the excitement of the anticipated invasion and the bad news about the Philippines, did not stir up half as much interest at Makapoo as Mast's loose pistol, once it became known generally that he had it. Everybody wanted it. In the first five days after the attack Mast had no less than seven separate offers to buy it, as well as two nocturnal attempts to steal it from him as he slept. He could not remember having had so much attention since he first came into this company over a year ago.

Quite plainly O'Brien had talked about it. About this free-floating, unrecorded pistol loose at Makapoo in Mast's hands. Out of his hunger for it, plus his lack of success in getting hold of it, O'Brien had talked about it to somebody, if not everybody. How else would anyone know? And Mast began to realize his error in having lied about it and said he'd bought it. He had done that out of sheer instinct, and because he did not want it brought to the attention of the supply room that he still had it; and after two years in the Army Mast was cynically suspicious that there existed more than one man who would go to the supply room and tell, just simply because he himself did not have one. And for the purpose he had used it, the lie had sufficed. The supply room apparently was still totally unaware it had a pistol missing. But in succeeding, the lie had created other problems. It had, in effect, thrown the possession of Mast's pistol open to the field: anyone who had it, owned it.

Actually, Mast was willing to accept possession of his pistol under those circumstances; or any other circumstances. Having worn and cared for it those days since the attack had made it his in a peculiar way that he could not possibly have felt that Sunday when he knew he had to turn it back in twenty-four hours. And from there, it was only one step to believing that he *had* bought it after all, the only logical step to take, in fact. He knew of course that somewhere there existed a paper with his signature on it saying that he owed God, or the Army, one pistol. And while the knowledge registered with him, it also somehow did not register. He *had* bought it. He could even, when pressed, remember the face of the man from the 8th Field Artillery who had sold it to him. So in one way the pistol had become what everyone believed it was. And Mast was prepared to defend it on those terms. From any source of jeopardy.

The offers to buy it ranged in price from twenty dollars to sixty dollars, none as high as the seventy dollars O'Brien had offered him under the stress of that first day. O'Brien himself was out of the bidding now, having lost nearly all of his seventy dollars in a poker game in one of the pill-boxes. Poker was just about the only recreational facility left them now, and since it was clear that money was not going to be of use to any of them for some time to come, almost everybody who had any cash played; and the young lieutenant in charge of the position was powerless to stop it. And usually, whenever anyone won a wad of money, the first thing they did was go to Mast and make an offer for his pistol. Mast, naturally, refused them all.

As for the two attempts to steal it, Mast was lucky in being able to circumvent them both. The first occurred on the third night after the attack. Up to then Mast had been used to sleeping with his cartridge belt, and the holstered pistol, under his head for a sort of makeshift pillow and he woke up from a fitful sleep in the unceasing ear-beating wind to feel his belt, with the pistol on it, being stealthily withdrawn from under his head. He made a grab for it, caught it and yanked, and retained his pistol. But when he raised up to look, all he could see in the moonless darkness was the retreating back of a crouched running figure, its footfalls silent because of the loudly buffeting wind. After that, he decided to sleep with his belt on, around his waist. And after someone, whose retreating back he could also see but not identify, tried two nights later to sneak the pistol out of its holster while he again slept, he slept after that with the pistol itself tucked into his waist belt under his buttoned-down shirt and zippered field jacket while still wearing the riflebelt outside. This made for difficult sleeping, but then sleeping at Makapoo was difficult at best, and he didn't care. Now that he had his pistol he meant to keep it.

It was interesting to speculate upon just why everyone was so desirous of possessing this particular pistol, and Mast did speculate on it, a little. Everybody had always wanted pistols, of course, but this was somehow becoming a different thing, he felt. But he was so busy working all day long, trying to sleep at night, and above all trying to keep and protect his pistol, that he really had very little time left to speculate on anything.

Certainly, a lot of it had to do with the fact that it was free, unattached. All the members of the machine-gun platoon at Makapoo carried pistols too, but theirs had been assigned to them and so nobody tried to steal them. It was pointless, because the serial numbers were registered to them. But because Mast had bought his (Had he? Yes! He had. He distinctly had.), instead of signing a requisition for it, it was unrecorded and therefore anyone who could come into possession of it would own it.

And yet, despite that very strong point, there seemed to be something else, something Mast, certainly, could not put his finger on. Everybody seemed to be getting frantic to possess his pistol. And Mast was unable to account for it, or understand it.

All Mast knew was the feeling that the pistol

gave him. And that was that it comforted him.
As he lay rolled up in his two blankets and one
shelterhalf at night with the rocky ground jab-
bing him in the ribs or flanks and the wind buffeting his head and ears, or as he worked his arms
numb to the shoulder all day long at the never-
ending job of putting up recalcitrant barbed wire,
it comforted him. Thy rod and thy staff. Perhaps
he had no staff—unless you could call his rifle
that—but he had a 'rod.' And it would be his salvation. One day it would save him. The sense of
personal defensive safety that it gave him was tremendous. He could even picture the scene: lying
wounded, and alone, his rifle lost, himself unable
to walk, and a Jap major bearing down on him
with a drawn saber to split him in half: then his
pistol would save him. The world was rocketing
to hell in a bucket, but if he could only hold onto
his pistol, remain in possession of the promise of
salvation its beautiful blue-steel bullet-charged
weight offered him, he could be saved.

CHAPTER THREE

The first open attempt, as distinguished from the nocturnal tries at stealing it, came from the same big, dark, inarticulate Irishman, O'Brien, who had tried to buy the pistol from Mast in the truck. It happened one night when Mast and he were on guard duty together a week after the attack. The tension brought on by the anticipated invasion still had not slacked off by then.

It was, of course, mandatory that at least one man should be awake at all times in each pill-box, or 'hole,' as they quickly came to be called, staring out over the darkling sea below the cliff in an eye-cracking effort to see Japanese landing craft where there were none. But in addition to these safeguards, because of the construction of the position and its vulnerability from the land side, a system of walking posts had been set up around the perimeter.

O'Brien, on this particular night, being from another 'hole,' happened to have the post adjoining Mast's, and during their two hours on post they met at the ends of their walkings and would stand for a while and talk in the chill, buffeting wind. It was during one of these meetings that they both thought they heard a sound, as of a stone falling, above the pummeling of the wind.

"What was that?" Mast whispered. "Did you hear that?"

"Yeah," O'Brien whispered back. "Yeah, I heard it."

They both had crouched down and now they listened a while longer but they heard nothing else. There was no moon and it was pitch black and impossible to see, but they both knew what was in front of them. The bare rock where they walked post went on perhaps ten yards in front of them, at which point there was a fence separating the rocky point from a field of thin soil and sparse grass owned by a white industrialist but operated for him by an industrious, silent Japanese man as a cattle feeding field. Just beyond the fence to the left the rock of the point rose steeply to what higher up became the top of a small mountain, while the field sloped away, far down to the highway on their right.

"It sounded like it came from right in there," Mast whispered, the wind whipping his words

away, and pointed to the spot where the rock began to rise above them.

"Yeah," O'Brien whispered, not too encourag-
ingly. "It sure did."

They listened some more.

"Well, what are we going to do?" Mast whispered finally.

"I don't know," O'Brien whispered. "What do
you think we ought to do?"

Mast was astonished. Big, tough O'Brien whom
he had seen engaged in so many heroic-sized fist-
fights asking *him* what to do. He was considerably
flattered. "Well, we can't just go back to walking
post without investigating it," he whispered
toughly, and drew his pistol. "Don't you think?"
he added.

"I guess so," O'Brien said without enthusiasm.
"But how'll we do it?"

Quietly Mast drew back the slide of the pistol
and let it scoop a shell up into the empty chamber into firing position. He put it on safety.

"You be careful of that damned thing, Mast,"
O'Brien whispered nervously.

"I will," Mast promised, and noted that he was
holding it rather gingerly himself. No one on the
position was allowed to carry a weapon with a
round actually loaded in the chamber, only in
the clip or magazine. And Mast couldn't help feeling guilty as if he were doing something wrong by
loading it. "Maybe it's only a cow?" he added as
an afterthought.

"Nah," O'Brien whispered. "They come and

took all five of them cows outta there a week ago."

"Then I'll have to take a look," Mast said toughly, but he nonetheless felt the same uneasy, vague nervousness he had felt the day of the attack and his back muscles had begun to twitch again. But he wasn't going to let O'Brien know that. "You cover me from here with your rifle. You got one in it?"

"No."

"Well, put one in. And for God's sake be careful with it. For God's sake don't shoot *me*."

In the deep dark, their faces only a few inches apart, and in spite of the evident nervousness on O'Brien's face, Mast could see a sudden, very subtle hint of craftiness come into the Irishman's pale green eyes.

"Tell you what," O'Brien whispered. "You gimme the pistol and let me go over and look and you cover me with your rifle."

Alarm for his pistol tingled all through Mast spontaneously, automatically. "Oh, no," he said quickly. "No. I don't mind. I'll do it."

"But I'm a lot bigger than you. And stronger."

"That doesn't matter as long as I got my pistol. Now look, you cover me. And for God's sake don't shoot me. I may be gone quite a while, so if you don't hear from me don't worry or shoot or anything."

"Don't worry, old pal," O'Brien whispered. "I'll be right here backing you up you get in any kind of trouble."

It made Mast feel very warm toward him, and

as he crawled off feeling quite brave, if a little nervous, he heard the quiet sound of the Springfield rifle bolt being withdrawn and levering a shell up into it.

Actually, it all came to nothing. At the fence, expecting to be shot in the face at any moment, Mast made himself stand up to climb it wishing now that he had let O'Brien borrow the pistol and do it. After that he crawled around in the field for perhaps five minutes being whipped in the face by the dried grass stems and getting seeds in his nose while his clothes got soaked from the dew. He saw nothing and heard nothing. Finally, he stood up, cautiously at first, and then walked back openly to the fence feeling foolish but still worried about O'Brien shooting him.

"It's me!" he called in a hoarse whisper. "For God's sake don't shoot me, now."

"Come on," O'Brien called softly.

It was Mast's first experience in combat against an enemy, if it could actually be called that, and he felt he had conducted himself very well. Even if it had turned out there wasn't any enemy. He also felt a great warmth of friendship for O'Brien, having shared this experience with him.

"What'd you find?" O'Brien said when he got back. He was still crouched down with his rifle.

"Nothing," Mast said in a normal voice. "It must have been just a piece of loose rock that fell off."

O'Brien unloaded his piece and stood up. He

laughed, still a little nervously, and slapped Mast on the back heavily. "I don't mind tellin' ya it sure made me nervous."

"Me too," Mast grinned warmly.

"But a pistol like that's perfect for that kind of a job," O'Brien said enviously.

"Sure is." Mast released the clip from it and then ejected the live shell in the chamber into the palm of his other hand, always an awkward procedure.

"Here, let me help you," O'Brien offered. "I'll hold it while you put the round back in the clip."

"Sure," Mast grinned and handed him the pistol. And that was when it happened. When Mast looked up from replacing the shell in the clip and held out his hand, it was to find O'Brien standing two paces off with the pistol stuck in his belt.

"Hey, come on," Mast protested, "Quit horsing around," and reached for his pistol. O'Brien stepped back a couple of more steps and stood grinning at him toothily and impudently.

"I got it now," he said. "And I mean to keep it. And whatta ya gonna do about it?"

"But you can't do something like that!" Mast said. He was deeply and sincerely shocked, if only at the sheer dishonesty, sheer trickery, of it. Only a moment before they had been warm buddies sharing a danger. He still could not believe O'Brien could really do it. He had to be joking. "You just can't!" he said.

"Can't I?" O'Brien grinned complacently. "I did, didn't I? And what you gonna do? You can't take it away from me. And you know it. You couldn't whip me in a fight, Mast." He grinned again. "So what are you gonna do?"

"I can turn you in to Sergeant Pender," Mast said, disliking himself for saying it; but a fury of blind rage, that worst of all angers which is the anger of outraged helplessness, was rising in him steadily.

O'Brien merely grinned. "For what? For taking a pistol off you that you ain't supposed to have? That pistol's not on the records, and you know it. You told me you bought it. So: that pistol was stole from the Army. By somebody. All's would happen would be Pender'd take it away from both of us." Once again, O'Brien grinned, toothily, and settled the pistol more firmly into his belt. "Anyway, you wouldn't turn me in and be a pigeon, would you now, Mast? 'Cause I'd have to beat hell outta you, then. And I don't want ta do that."

Mast stood rooted, every moral ethic in him violated. Not only to have done it by such a sneaky subterfuge, but to have done it immediately after they had warmly shared a danger that might have been truly serious, was incredible. It was inconceivable to him. And then to threaten him with a beating, too! Because it was true that he would stand no chance in a fist fight with O'Brien, no chance at all. Helpless outrage flamed all through Mast.

"Maybe you can beat me up. And maybe you will. But at least you won't get to keep that pistol, I promise you that. It's mine. And I bought it. And I want it back."

"Ah, come on now, Mast. You don't mean that. Come on, you might as well give me the holster and the clips. They won't do you no good without the pistol."

"You'll never get them. You'll have to take them off me first, if you do. And I'll throw them over the cliff first." The thought of his pistol gone, taken, no longer his, and taking with it his margin of safety, his chance of being saved, brought a hollow, sick feeling to the pit of Mast's stomach. "Of all the dirty, sneaking, lying, cheating, low-down, sneakthieves in the world, you're the worst, O'Brien. You take the cake." But the words were useless, worse than useless. What were words?

O'Brien apparently felt the same thing, because he merely grinned at Mast. "Call me anything you want. Come on, gimme them clips and holster."

"No."

O'Brien shrugged. "Okay. I can pick some up someplace else. I got the important thing, and that's the pistol.

"Look, Mast. I'll try to be reasonable with you. And you try to be reasonable. Okay?" O'Brien squared his shoulders, patted his new pistol, grinned briefly, and settled himself to talk intelligently. "You don't need this pistol, Mast. What do you need this pistol for? You're a rear-rank rudy in the third squad a the third platoon. A ordinary rifleman. I'm the first scout in my platoon. You know what that means? I'll be the first guy in, anywhere we go, me and my partner the second scout. I'm the guy who'll be sneaking through the brush getting my ass shot off. What if I got captured? Did you ever see them Samurai sabers them Jap officers carry? You know what they do to prisoners? They cut them in two with them sabers. And I'm the first scout. I really *need* this pistol. It might be just the extra edge might save my life someday. It might really actually save my life, save *me*." O'Brien paused weightily, to let this sink in. "You realize what that means? to a first scout?" He paused again. "While look at you: a rear-rank rudy of a rifleman with a education: with a education yet! Why, you might even be working in the orderly room someday. You might be. You might really be working in the orderly room. So what do you need with this pistol?" He stopped and plumped his knuckles powerfully on his hips, his argument complete.

Mast listened to him with outraged, furious astonishment. O'Brien really thought he had a right to his, Mast's, pistol. Had a right to just take it. O'Brien had convinced himself he was morally right in his barefaced thievery. Not only morally right, but righteous, he was! And what was more, he really *believed* it. Furiously, ardently, Mast wished he was big enough or strong enough to whip him, to beat him up, and *take* his pistol back. But he wasn't.

"Now, I'd like to be fair with you, Mast," O'Brien said. "I really would. Hell, I'd even *give* you ten bucks for it, if I hadn't lost almost all my money playing poker, I really would. Now, be a good boy, and gimme them clips and holster."

"You'll never get them." Suddenly an idea struck Mast, a clever idea. He had seen it in a movie once. He might not be able to whip O'Brien, but there was no reason he couldn't outsmart him. Making himself look defeated, Mast stepped back and turned around to pick up his rifle where it lay alongside O'Brien's. "And don't think you can take them off me," he said. "If you try, I'll buttstroke you so help me God." Bending to pick up his rifle as he spoke, he caught it at the balance with his right hand and at the same time picked up a large, loose rock with his left, concealing it against his leg. Then he stepped back, dejectedly.

"Don't worry," O'Brien grinned at him toothily. "I can awys git clips." He sidled up to his own rifle. "Just you don't try nothing yourself, that's all. I wouldn't want to have to sock you. But as for buttstroking a guy," he said righteously, "I myself wouldn't never even considra doing something like that to a guy who was on my own country's side in this war." He grinned, and confident of his physical superiority turned his face away from Mast, down toward where his rifle lay, offering his back.

It was Mast's moment, the one Mast had hoped for. Quickly, he lifted his left arm and tossed the heavy rock as if putting a shot, off over O'Brien's head toward the fence, then shifted his rifle to his left hand to be ready. The rock crashed down on the rocky slope, making a loud noise they could hear even above the buffeting of the wind, and O'Brien leaped up crouching, bringing up his rifle.

"What was that?" he whispered.

"Did you hear it too?" Mast whispered. He took one step forward quietly and bending forward a little, reached with his right hand in under O'Brien's right arm that was holding the pistol-grip of his rifle up at the ready. He snatched his pistol back, out of O'Brien's belt, and backed off with it.

O'Brien spun around and looked at Mast disbelievingly.

"Don't come near me," Mast said. "Or I'll brain you with it. Sure as hell." He nodded in answer to the unspoken question. "Yes, it was me. I tossed that rock out over your head."

Slowly O'Brien swung his massive head around toward where the rock had fallen, then swung it back again, his pale green eyes staring at Mast. "You dirty bastard!" he said furiously. For a moment it looked as though he might lay his rifle down and charge. "You dirty, sneaking, cheating bastard!" But the upraised pistol in Mast's hand ready to mash down on him was clearly too much odds to give away to any man.

"Come on," Mast taunted, gaining confidence from O'Brien's hesitation. "Come on, O'Brien. You want my pistol, I'll give it to you:—Right in the jaw." All his frustrated outrage and helpless fury of before boiled up in him, and for a moment he wished O'Brien really would come on, so he could smash him with it.

O'Brien straightened up leisurely and set his rifle-butt on the bare rock underfoot and leaned on the muzzle, an attempt of a nonchalance that did not entirely come off. "Smart guy!" was all he said. "Goddamn smart guy!" But the chagrin and sense of loss he felt couldn't be entirely hidden. In just the short space he had had it, had felt it there, securely, in his belt, the pistol had obviously become his. It was his own pistol he had lost back to Mast.

"Smarter than you, at any rate," Mast said, and allowed himself a grin. "By any counts. Now get on back to your own damned post and walk it like you're supposed to do and get off of mine. Thief."

"Go to hell, smart guy," O'Brien sneered. But he went. "Just watch out, smart guy, that's all," he called back ominously.

"I'll watch," Mast called. "Especially you I'll watch."

Happily, just simply physiologically content at possessing it once again, but at the same time burning with fury and violated ethics whenever he thought of what O'Brien had tried to pull, Mast rubbed his pistol affectionately for a few moments and inspected it, feeling creep over him again comfortingly that sense of possible salvation, of that extra little margin which people without pistols didn't have, that chance of being saved. Sheer horror assailed him when he thought of how close he really had come to losing it. He worked the slide back and forth a couple of times, as he had been so carefully taught by the Army, to make sure there was no forgotten round in the chamber, then slammed the cartridge-heavy clip back up into the butt, then hefted it in his hand.

It was really beautiful, by God! As an afterthought Mast pulled out of his hip pocket the oily issue handkerchief he kept there for going over both his weapons, and he rubbed the pistol all over vigorously with it. He wanted to get any taint of O'Brien's greasy, sweat-salty hands off it.

Mast realized clearly, for perhaps the first time, just how very careful he was going to have to be from now on, not to lose it. Those seven or eight offers to buy it, plus the two nocturnal attempts to steal it, should have prepared him for what happened tonight with O'Brien. That had been a gross error, and he had not been prepared. But he would be prepared from now on. The pistol would not only not get out of his sight from now on, it would not even get out of his hands. Nobody would trick Mast again.

Toughly, confidently, Mast slapped it back down into its holster and latched the flap shut over it. He slung his rifle and resumed walking his post, repeating over his promise to himself.

CHAPTER FOUR

It was a few days after the episode with O'Brien that the supply room clerk, who had issued Mast the pistol in the first place and whose name was Musso, came out to the Makapuu Head position for the first time. His supply room had been set up in a couple of tents at the company command post, and Mast and the others at Makapoo had not seen him since the day of the attack. He came to bring two new aircooled .50-caliber machine guns, the first Mast's company had ever had, which the company commander had decided were to be set up in the two most important pillboxes at Makapoo, the company's most important position. Up to then they had had only the .30-caliber watercooled to repel invasion.

Mast knew he was coming with them, of course. Everyone knew about the new guns. And it worried Mast considerably: What if Musso remembered the pistol he had refused to have back the day of the attack? Mast knew, by gossip from the kitchen trucks, which on most days were the only outside contact Makapoo had with the world, that the other three men who had been on guard with him that Sunday had finally been returned to the company. Mast had, in fact, made a point of finding out about them. Presumably, since they were delivered to the company CP from Schofield en masse, they had been required to turn in their pistols and other guard equipment before they were distributed off to their assigned beach positions. If so, Mast could only reason that such would be the logical time for someone to come out from the command post to pick up his pistol, too. But no one had come. Why? Had his been overlooked, as he had hoped? And if so, what if Musso came out with the big fifties and saw Mast still wearing his guard pistol? Where could Mast hide it? that it would be safe? And anyway, what if Musso only saw Mast himself? without the pistol? Might he not even then still remember? And demand it?

It was an almost impossible thought, Mast's mind just simply balked and refused to accept it, that he might now, at this late date, after becoming so used to it, be forced to give up his little margin of safety, his slight chance of being saved over men who did not have pistols, his heavy powerful beautiful bluenosed savior, which would be his salvation.

Mast brooded over this considerably after he learned Musso was coming with the new guns. It was a strange double reaction that he had, because while he knew he had got the pistol from Musso and his supply room, he could also distinctly remember now that he had bought it. And if he felt a frightened guilt at the way he knew he really had come by his salvation, he also felt a radiant happiness over the other way, the way which he had convinced himself he had come by it. He not only could call up at will now the face of the man from the 8th Field Artillery from whom he had bought it, he could remember the exact transaction that took place and the exact spot and scene where it was consummated. He clung to this and just simply forgot Musso.

So when Mast came up out of the uppermost, or number six, hole where he had been on post at one of the machine guns, and saw far down, below him on the highway the little weapons carrier with Musso in the front beside the driver and the long snouts of the fifties sticking up in back, he suffered a strange mixed double feeling which quickly turned into a definite fright.

Actually, during those few days from the incident with O'Brien to the coming of Musso, Mast had had almost no trouble at all where the pistol was concerned. There had been no more nocturnal attempts to steal it, since everyone knew by now that Mast slept with it in his waist belt and buttoned down under his shirt. And there had been only three offers to buy it from him, two of them by former would-be buyers who had won at poker and were coming back with a higher offer.

But other than this it had been a quiet few days for Mast and his pistol, and now as he stood outside the number six hole and watched the arrival of the two fifties and Musso, he suffered what, for lack of any stronger term, could only be called a genuine traumatic experience.

The little weapons carrier apparently had only just stopped, because Musso had not even climbed out of it yet. As Mast watched from high up on the rocky point, the tiny figure of the tall, lanky, aging Italian unraveled its long legs from the seat well and ambled over to where the sentry at the gate in the wire was opening it. Unlatched, the two of them dragged aside the post fastened to the hanks of loose wire and accordion rolls which made up the gate, and the little weapons carrier followed Musso in, and then they yelled up the hill to the number one hole which in addition to its guns was used also for the young lieutenant's command post.

Mast's eyes followed Musso, almost hypnotized. He could not help seeing the Italian oldtimer as his personal and vindictive enemy. If Mast's pistol was his savior, and his potential salvation, then Musso was Satan, the Devil, come to take it away. Mast could only hate him; viciously, bitterly, terrifiedly and with horror. On the other hand, Musso was a visitor to the position from the outside world beyond the wire, contact with which had been denied them except for the kitchen trucks, and Mast's instinct was to rush up to him and shake his hand happily and ask him what news there was, how was it going in the Philippines? The two emotions pushed and shoved at each other inside Mast, battling each other over the no-man's land of his body, while Mast himself only stood and stared, transfixed, hypnotized, by this Evil that was climbing the hill with long-legged strides toward the lieutenant's hole, and at the same time there appeared in front of his face that other face of the man from the 8th Field Artillery talking cunningly and grinning slyly as he tried to milk another five dollars out of Mast for the pistol.

There was, of course, only one thing for him to do. That was to get out of sight and keep out of sight until Musso left. Re-enforcing his highly sensible decision, there was running through Mast's mind still another picture, like a short strip of movie film being run over and over and over again without pause, and this was the antithetical filming of his salvation by pistol: the same Jap major was once again rushing down on him with the same bejeweled, gleaming, beautiful Samurai sword through the same jungle on the same unknown island, and the same Mast lay, alone, with the same wound, and missing the same lost rifle, only this time there was no pistol. As a result, as Mast watched the other Mast struggle up to a sitting position, the Jap major, leaping astraddle the wounded legs, his two-handed saber describing a flashing gleaming beautiful arc and striking just beside the neck, clove the sitting Mast splitting him in two to the waist as Mast had seen done to Chinese prisoners in news photos, and the still-living Mast looked down and with anguish watched one half of his own body fall away from the other half while Mast himself anguishedly watched him. Over and over the little film vignette entitled *Ordeal Without Pistol* ran itself through his mind without pause, and Mast stood hopelessly and watched himself divided by saber uncounted numbers of times.

But where was he to get out of sight? The quickest would be to go right back down into number six hole where he had just been relieved, but to do that would be to invite all kinds of suspicion. No man in his right mind would remain in one of these wretched holes and sit and chat with his relief after he had been relieved. The only other alternative was to go down to the number four hole, Mast's home hole where all his gear was, and sit there on his barracks bag and hope no one called him.

It was an unsatisfactory alternative, but it was the only one. Of course he did not make it. Even if there had been enough time to get there without being seen, he had already sacrificed it by standing and staring at Musso and the picture of his, Mast's, own frightful future. Long before he had climbed down to the entrance of the number four hole he was spotted by old Sergeant Pender, the chief noncom of the position, and called down to help upload the machine guns, as he had known he would be.

Reluctantly, miserably, but with no alternative left him now, Mast climbed down past the already lost security of the number four hole, which he looked at longingly, to where the five or six men who had been called out to help unload the guns were converging on the weapons carrier. As he scrambled down over the rough rocks, it seemed to Mast that all his life as far back as he could remember he had lived the life of a doomed and guilty man, for some obscure reason he had never been able to isolate, and that this was just one more classic example of it: These other five or six men, they had nothing to be frightened or afraid of or guilty about in going to help unload the carrier; only he, Mast, did. They could approach it happily or cheerfully or laughing or joking without guilty consciences; only he, Mast, could not. And almost every event that had happened to him in his life had been the same way, and never once had any of them been his own fault. Any more than this one now was his own fault: he had not stolen the pistol. Why this was so, Mast could not understand; but it always had been, and Mast could not help wondering with the apathy of despair, as he approached the weapons carrier down on the level ground, if it would continue to be so through the rest of his life, too. Must he always be doomed and guilty and if so, why? Mast wondered as he approached them.

It was an ordeal the like of which Mast hoped never to have to go through again in his life, that unloading. Musso did not recognize the pistol, in fact he apparently did not even see it, but that did not mean that at the very next moment he might not do so. So for the forty-five minutes it took to unload the two heavy guns from the little truck and carefully cart them and their tripods up the rough, rocky hillside and set them up in the holes to which they had been assigned, Mast existed in a state of suspense that all but unmanned him. As he first came up Musso grinned and said hello to him, and he said hello to Musso. There wasn't much choice. And after that he tried always to unobtrusively keep someone or some thing between himself and Musso. Musso stood beside the truck with old Sergeant Pender, leaning on it and supervising everything and making sure they were careful not to drop or dent or scratch his precious new guns, and after they got them off the truck and began struggling up the treacherous slope with them, he followed them there too, do-ing the same thing. And to Mast's eyes, which to Mast seemed to bulge and roll around giddily with this unbearable suspense, Musso with his thin, cynical, Italian old-soldier's face was the living picture of Evil. To say that Mast hated him would be such an understatement as to lose all

conveyance of meaning. Mast hated him viciously, murderously, with the white purity of Galahad
and every fiber of his existence.

It was only some time, a full half hour at least,
after Musso left, and after Mast himself had gone
off by himself and sat with his head in his hands
on a rock, that Mast was actually able to realize
he still had his pistol after all. He was so shaken
by his ordeal that, even when he did realize it, it
did not mean anything. Finally, though, he
was able to appreciate it: He had gone through
the ordeal, and now his salvation was his. *Truly*
his. His pistol was his, free and clear.

Obviously, the paper he had signed had been
lost, perhaps in the packing and moving out from
Schofield. Or maybe it had been lost after they got
down here. But the requisition obviously had to
be lost. And just as obviously, Musso himself had
clearly forgotten all about it. Mast had walked
right past him with it hanging on his hip and Musso had looked right at it and hadn't noticed or
remembered.

So his pistol was his, truly and actually his, perhaps for the first time. Once again the face of the
man from the 8th Field Artillery from whom he
had bought it, and the scene where he had bought
it, and the conversation of the transaction itself,
all unfolded itself in his mind. It was living
proof that it was his, now; that he had bought it
after all. When Mast raised his head from his
hands, the whole world had taken on a different

look, a new look, as if he had never seen it before, or as if it were sparkling cheerfully after a clean, refreshing rain.

Mast's salvation, Mast's chance of surviving, Mast's little margin of safety which riflemen without pistols did not have, just as machine gunners with pistols but without rifles did not have it either, was Mast's again, really Mast's. Now all he had to do was keep it. Keep it away from these maniacal wolves on this Makapoo beach position who wanted to take it from him.

CHAPTER FIVE

The next attempt against Mast's pistol came ten days after the supply clerk Musso had visited them to bring the guns.

By now, almost three weeks after the Pearl Harbor attack, the initial invasion scare had tapered off and things had settled down at Makapoo considerably. Obviously if the Japanese were going to follow up their air attack with an immediate invasion, they would have done so within three weeks. Also, at Makapoo almost all of the heavy, basic barbed wire work had been completed and all that remained to be done were the small jobs of touching up and adding refinements here and there; and it was this fact that had to do with the, one might say, flanking attack against Mast's pistol when it came.

Mast had been working, whenever he was not

on post at the guns, with a large twelve-man detail under one of the buck sergeant squad leaders, putting up combinations of single- and double-apron wire around the three sides of the position that did not face the sea. This was one of the major wiring jobs, and on this detail also happened to be Mast's old enemy O'Brien as well as another man, a thin-faced little corporal and assistant squad leader named Winstock, who, when he himself was not on post commanding one of the holes, was in charge of one half of the wire detail.

Because this was a major, and important, wiring job, each man's time was staggered so that no matter who was on post at the machine guns during the day, there were still always twelve men available for the wire detail. As a result, Mast would often find himself working side by side with his old enemy O'Brien. Since O'Brien had tried to take Mast's pistol himself, Mast and he had not spoken and avoided each other whenever possible. But O'Brien, in his deliberately buffoonish, obviously self-advancing way, had become quite friendly with Winstock on the detail. And after the heavy, basic work was completed and the large detail broken up, Mast was assigned to a smaller detail of four men under Winstock, which also included O'Brien, to do some of the touching-up work. That, really, was what became Mast's undoing.

It was unbelievably hard work, that heavy, main

labor of putting up double-apron and single-apron fence around the entire position. There were at least three hundred and fifty to four hundred yards of it to do, and just a few inches under the soil of all this ground was an almost solid sheet of rock. The screw-type iron pickets, standard in the Army since the trench warfare of the first World War in France, could no more be screwed into it than the wooden tentpegs for the infantry sheltertents could be driven into it. The long stretch of double-apron they had put up during the first days on the public beach below and at right angles to the rocky point of the position itself, had been satisfying, almost pleasant, rewarding work—even if the sea had washed it out twice before the sergeant in charge learned to put it back from the high tide mark. All that was needed there was an iron or wooden bar to thrust through the eye of the picket for leverage to screw it down in the firm, yielding sand, and the pickets, long and short, had gone up in long straight even lines satisfying to the eye and to the esthetic sense. That was wiring as the textbook drawings showed it.

But here, with the bedrock just beneath the surface, and thrusting up through it in so many places, the wiring work was tragic and foredoomed, not pleasing or satisfying at all, and infinitely more exhausting. But they got it done. Picks were delivered to them on the kitchen trucks, after being requisitioned on the field telephone, and where nothing else availed holes were dug for the pickets in the solid rock, then the broken rubble jammed back in around the picket's screw. At other places cracks and fissures in the rock itself could be utilized and pickets could be wedged into them. The result was a straggly, unevenly spaced, often crooked line of wire and crazily tilted pickets, many of which would have pulled out or fallen over at the first healthy yank. And the weight of a falling human body would have uprooted at least three of the major, long pickets, to say nothing of the shorter anchor pickets.

Nevertheless, they did get it done. At an incredible cost in backbreaking labor. Mast would go to bed at night, if rolling up in two blankets and one shelterhalf in the never-ceasing wind could be called going to bed, unshaven, grimy, unwashed, fat rolls of dirt pressing distastefully up under all his fingernails and hardly able to stand the smell of his own body, with his arms and back aching dully and unceasingly like long-abscessed teeth, and knowing that in six hours he would be called to do a night guard stint. Sometimes he would wake up with both arms totally numb to the shoulders, so that if he were not careful, his own uncontrollable thumb would fall down and stick him in the eye. He was not alone in all this, either. However, knowing that he was not alone in his suffering did not make him any the less unhappy about it. And it was at such times that the feel of the pistol tucked in his belt was the greatest, if not the only comfort he had in living.

No one on the position, excepting only the young lieutenant of course, who could go into the company command post whenever he required, had had a shave or bath since the war had started. Locked-in in their own little island of barbed wire ironically constructed by themselves, cut off from the world entirely except for the daily three deliveries of their food and water, they grew steadily dirtier and more ratty-looking, and more depressed. With the tapering off of the threat of immediate invasion the solid unity its possibility had forced upon them slowly died, and irascibility flourished. It was not until the end of the third week that, freed now of the press of more militarily important matters, someone at the company CP thought of the idea of running a shuttle system of trucks in to the CP where there was running water, so that once every two or three days each man could get in for a shower and a shave. It did a great deal for the morale at Makapoo. It did a great deal for the morale of all of the company's isolated positions. But it was also the bathing shuttle system that proved to be Mast's undoing with the pistol.

It had been decided, by whom and with what logic no one seemed to know, that four men were the most that could be spared from Makapoo at any one time. Other positions with complements of only ten men could spare three, but whyever the decision, arbitrary or not, four was the rule for Makapoo. And when it came Mast's turn to go, Corporal Winstock's little wire-repair detail was sent in together under the command of Winstock.

They rode in, the four of them, in the big two-and-a-half-ton personnel truck, which on its way picked up also the quota of shavers and bathers from the company's other isolated and waterless positions between Makapoo and the CP. This was the first time any of these men had seen each other since the war began, and they talked to each other eagerly like old long-lost friends, although in actual fact back before the war none of them had been much more than casual acquaintances. Red-eyed, dirty and unshaven, they huddled together in the back of the open truck as if for mutual protection and stared out hungrily at the scattered civilian homes they passed. As the truck drew closer to the city, the thinly scattered homes became a little thicker, and whenever they passed a spot where they knew one of the company's positions to be, they speculated enviously on the civilian homes nearby, if there were any, wondering if there were daughters in them and whether or not the occupants drank liquor. If there weren't any civilian homes nearby, the truck would stop and pick up another quota of bathers.

The company's command post was located at the foot of another headland which was shaped like a humpbacked whale and was known as Koko Head. To the eyes of tourists on a cruise ship at sea, when such things had still existed, it did indeed look like a whale. Just across its low saddle which separated it from the mountains behind, and through which the highway ran, the outskirts of the city began a few hundred yards beyond. Here were girls and whiskey both, and here was the other half of the company's sector, the 'gravy train' half, with most of its positions located on rich beach estates.

But long before the truck even reached the top of this saddle, where these riches at least would have become visible to them, it turned off to the left down a curving side road. Here, nestled at the foot of Koko Head, was a park area which formerly had been a sort of public state park. At the foot of a crumbling fifty-foot cliff into which steps had been cut was a beautiful little palm-studded beach for swimming in a sheltered little inlet known as Hunauma Bay, complete with even a dancehall-bar and little restaurant, now closed and silent and sad. At the top of the cliff in the park area, set back in a sparsely planted grove of thorn trees which provided perfect camouflage as well as sheltering shade, were the tents of the company's command post. Not far away in the same grove were the two public bath houses, for men and for women, but both of them now used by the troops at hand. It was toward these that the truck with Mast and the others on it headed.

Mast, who had almost forgotten a shower and shave could feel so luxurious, was careful to hang his cartridge belt with the holstered pistol on it in full view of the open shower stall, and after he finished his ablutions and dressed he went down the cliff and sat by himself on the steps of the deserted dancehall, so hollowly empty now, luxuriating in the strange, warm, sunny quiet which the absence of the Makapoo wind made to sound so loud in his ears, while the shuttered-up silence of the dancehall-bar and restaurant behind him, where civilians were no longer allowed to come, afflicted him with a hungry melancholy. Mast had not realized how used to that wind he had become.

It was here that little Corporal Winstock, his perpetually sly look still upon his thin rodent-like face, sought him out and sat down beside him. Even then, Mast had wondered why.

"Sure is nice, ain't it?" Winstock said, smiling craftily and looking out under the palms at the peaceful, sunny bay whose quiet water rippled and glinted in the sunshine. "Hell, I thought I was deaf, by God, when I first got here outta that wind." He rubbed his hand lingeringly over his freshly shaved, sharp chin. "Sure wish they hadn't of closed the jookjoint, don't you?" he added sorrowfully.

"Yeah," Mast said. "It's hell to think of having to go back out there again, ain't it?" he added absently. He was emotionally blanked out too, like the rest of them, here in this quiet sheltered place.

"Whyn't you get yourself a job in the orderly room?" Winstock said craftily. "With your education. Then y'could stay here all the time." He got up lazily and went down the dancehall steps and out onto the closely clipped grass that led down to the sand beach under the palms, and walked around to Mast's right side.

"I don't want a job in the orderly room," Mast said.

Winstock had stopped and was standing looking at Mast. "Hey, Mast! I never knew you had a pistol. How come? When you're a rifleman. You ain't supposed to have a pistol."

That Winstock could stand there and barefacedly say such a thing was immediately suspicious to Mast. Winstock could not have failed to notice the pistol during the past three weeks. Everyone on the position knew about it, excepting only the young lieutenant and the two platoon sergeants who were in charge. Certainly Winstock would have heard about it from O'Brien. Mast turned to look at the crafty face carefully.

"I bought it off a guy from the 8th Field who had it and wanted to sell it, back before the war," he said.

"No kiddin'!" Winstock exclaimed with great surprise. "You're lucky!" Then he rubbed his newly shaved chin again, thoughtfully. "But that's buyin' and receiving stolen property, ain't it? That guy, or somebody, 'course it might not of been him, had to steal that pistol." Again he paused, then wrinkled up his crafty face into a rueful look. "Gee, I don't know what I ought to do about that, Mast." It was the first time Mast could remember hearing Winstock use the word 'Gee.' Usually Winstock swore explosively.

"What do you mean: 'Do'?" Mast said, his suspicions rising further.

"Well, *you* know." Winstock shrugged apologetically. "That's an Army pistol, you know. 'Course you yourself are innocent, *I* know that. But however *you* got it, and however that guy who *sold* it to you got it, in the beginning *some*body had to *steal* it—and from the *Ar*my. Now what kind of a position does that put *me* in?"

"It doesn't put you in any kind of a position, as far as I can see," Mast said narrowly.

"It don't? Oh, but it does, Mast; it does. Don't you see? You're in my detail and I'm in charge of you. That makes it my responsibility. Not only to myself but to the Army too. Don't you see that?"

"What the hell?" Mast growled. "You're not in command of me. I'm not even in the same platoon you are. My squad leader's the guy that's in command of me. I'm only under you temporarily, on a little temporary detail, to do a definite, temporary job."

"That's just my point," Winstock said. " 'Course it's only temporary, and as long as you're there, long as you're in my detail, you're my responsibility, and so: so is that pistol." He paused again and stared off thoughtfully, and rubbed again that freshly shaven chin that he, like Mast, was obviously still unused to. "I'm just going to have to figure out what to do, I guess. That's all."

"Do?" Mast growled nervously. "Do! What the hell do you mean: *Do?*"

"Well, whether to make you turn it over to me," Winstock shrugged apologetically, "and turn it in. It puts me in a hell of a position, Mast. I don't mind telling you." He looked sad.

"Why, you're crazy!" Mast exploded, and jumped up convulsively. He stood staring at Winstock a moment and then sat back down again. "You're not in command of me in the first place! And in the second, it's none of your damned business anyway, this pistol! It has nothing to do with *our* company! I told you: I bought it off a guy in the 8th Field!"

"Well, that's not the way I see it," Winstock said sadly. "I see it like it's a sort of a responsibility of ethics—like, Mast, you know? I just got to decide what I ought to do.

"Well, I'll let you know. Soon's I figure it out. Got to think about it." He slapped Mast on the arm, warmly and apologetically. "I'm sorry, kid. Well, maybe I'll feel like I won't have to do it maybe.

"Well, come on. We better get back upstairs. The truck'll be ready to leave soon."

"So you'll let me know?" Mast growled sourly.

"Sure," Winstock said cheerfully, "sure. Soon's I figure out what I oughta do." He turned and started off across the grass toward the steps up the cliff.

Mast continued to sit, staring out at the water framed by the softly rustling palms, but the beautiful scene had lost a great deal of its appeal for him. He could not remember Winstock being that kind of a chicken noncom; usually it was just the reverse, and Winstock was always in trouble from trying to work angles. Nervously Mast cracked his knuckles, one by one methodically, and at the same time convulsively, then bit a hangnail off his right index finger and spat it out angrily. He should never have come down here where Winstock could accost him openly. He should have stayed where there were other people. Winstock wouldn't have dared do such a thing in front of other people. The pistol was becoming an almost unbearable responsibility. Everything he did or thought had to be governed by it. He could hardly keep up with it all.

From the top of the stairs in the cliff, Winstock hollered down at him to come on, that the truck was loading, and as he got up wearily to go, he looked at the lovely tropic scene before him, the like of which he had seen in so many movies and had so often dreamed of seeing in the reality; it left him feeling only an intense, gloomy sense of tragedy and sorrow, and a sad, resigned melancholy. This was not for him, any more than were the 'gravy train' positions of the other half of the company's sector. For him in life there were only the Makapoos and the Winstocks. There was an almost enjoyable luxury in accepting and admitting it.

The ride back out to Makapoo was even worse. Everyone hated leaving the comforts and shelter of the CP, meager as they were, compared to the beach positions in the city. When the truck left the cover of the Koko Head saddle and came back out to the beach, the unceasing wind began to buffet them again. Up in front, right behind the cab where the most shelter was, Winstock and O'Brien sat opposite each other with their heads together talking and grinning at each other. Far off across the open sea here, its surf whipped up by the wind, Molokai where Stevenson had lived and where the leper colony still was, was visible as a low storm cloud on the horizon.

There was no real doubt in Mast's mind as to what Winstock would decide to do. Nonetheless, after the truck had deposited them back within their isolated barbed-wire island at Makapoo and the little four-man detail had gone right back to work straightening and strengthening pickets and trying to dress up the hopelessly uneven lines of wire, Mast spent the rest of the day in an absolute agony of suspense, before Winstock finally came around to him after chow that evening.

"I've thought it over, Mast," Winstock said, his thin, sharp little face twisted up with apology.

"Thought it over carefully. And I'm gonna have to take your pistol and turn it in to Sergeant Pender to be turned in to the supply room.

"I hate to have to do it, Mast," he said, "and I know you'll think it's chicken. But my conscience just won't let me do anything else. It's my responsibility as a noncom. Maybe this way someday it'll get back to its rightful owner," he said piously.

Mast stared at him in silence with narrowed eyes, his mind casting frantically about this way and that to try and find some escape. There wasn't any. Whatever else, Winstock was a corporal with authority. All he had to do if Mast refused was go to Sergeant Pender anyway. Whatever old Sergeant Pender thought, he would always back up a corporal against a private. Slowly he took off his rifle cartridge belt and unhooked the pistol from it and passed it over.

"I'll take the extra clips, too," Winstock said.

Mast passed them over.

"I'm sure sorry, Mast," Winstock said, squinting his face up apologetically.

" 'Sall right," Mast said.

He stood and stared after the wiry little corporal as he made his way down toward the number one CP hole with the stuff. The man, all unwitting, because of some impractical, obscure, personal moral point, was carrying off Mast's hope, more than his hope: his faith; and Mast could have, and would have, easily killed him, had there been any way at all of getting by with it.

Mast had passed one day of horrible anxiety, and was to pass a number more of almost suicidal depression. When you take away a man's chance of being saved, Mast asked himself over and over as the little movie of the Jap major splitting him in twain like a melon returned to plague him day after day, when you do that to a man, what is there left?

But the one day of horrible anxiety, and the number more of near suicidal depression, were as nothing to what Mast felt just one week later when, going out on another detail after Winstock's wire-repair detail had been disbanded, Mast saw Corporal Winstock wearing on his own rifle belt Mast's pistol.

CHAPTER SIX

What had caused Winstock to do it, to come parading out in the open with the pistol so soon after he had won it, was something that would probably never be known. Certainly at the time Mast was in no state to speculate on it.

In any case Winstock, after forcing himself (with who knew what monumental efforts of will power) to wait a whole week, apparently could stand it no longer and finally had had to begin wearing it. And who knew what anguished arguments with himself he may have gone through in making his decision?

Mast of course was thinking, and indeed was concerned with, none of these things. Such spasms of outrage, fury and hate flamed and exploded and smouldered all through him that his psyche, had it been visible, might have resembled an artillery barrage seen at night, and Mast himself swore he could smell the odor of ozone in his nostrils. He had not been put today on the same detail with Winstock, who had been given charge of a smaller detail to police the edge of the highway outside the wire, so all Mast really got was a glimpse as his own detail was marched out through the gate of wire which the sentry closed after them. But the glimpse was enough. There wasn't, of course, anything he could do about it then. Mast was not at all sure there was anything he could do about it ever.

The new detail Mast had been assigned to was not a permanent, or even a semi-permanent one, but was a one shot, a one day's job.

Back in October and November, when Mast's company had been building the pillboxes they now manned, across the highway from them a little farther down an engineer company had been blasting and digging a cave in the cliff. This cliff, of black volcanic rock, ran straight up ninety or a hundred feet, and was the shoulder of the mountain range behind it. At one time the mountain shoulder must have descended at this point to the sea, but now a shelf had been blasted out to give the highway passage around it. Down this cliff the highway descended steeply in a curve to come out onto the great flat hollow of the Kaneohe Valley. The strategists of the Hawaiian Department had chosen this spot to place a huge demolition of high explosives which when detonated would tumble the tip end of the mountain down over the highway and on down into the sea, to block the highway. That was the purpose of the cave the engineer company had blasted into the cliff in October. It was really one vast mine.

The strategy of this plan, as every man at Makapoo knew, centered around the fact that an enemy (which back in October had to remain nameless and amorphous but could now openly be called the Japanese) would probably attempt his main landings on the beaches of the Kaneohe Valley where the reefs were low and the beach was good. This highway here at Makapoo and the highway up over the much more famous Pali, which had been mined also, were the only two roads over the mountains into Honolulu, and if both roads were blown, the enemy would be bottled up in the Kaneohe Valley and forced to go north and around the mountains and come down the center of the island.

That was the strategy. However, the idea of leaving several tons of high explosive lying around ready to go off at any moment was disturbing to the strategists. In peacetime, they could not quite bring themselves to do this. There might even have been political repercussions, if they had. Also, it was not inconceivable that saboteurs might want to blow it up to aid the enemy. Such a demolition, once constructed and completed, became a physical fact, rather than a mere idea. And as an existing fact it could be equally as useful to the enemy as to the ones who built it, depending upon the tactical situation existing at the time. The demolition might easily, and suddenly, turn into its own opposite and become a danger rather than an aid.

So, for all of these reasons, the demolition had not been loaded back in peacetime. Then, when the attack came, and immediate invasion was expected, there were too many other things of pressing importance. So the big, empty, manmade cave had simply stood there, hollowly. And now, more than a month after the initial attack and confusion, someone had remembered it. The threat of immediate invasion was past, but the threat of future invasion in heavy force was not. So it had been decided at this late date to go ahead and load the demolition.

That was the detail Mast, along with a number of other men from Makapoo, was on that day. Trucks came from the underground vaults in the city loaded down with cases of high explosive. The small engineer detail at the cave, which could not possibly handle so much weight to be moved, had been instructed to get aid from Mast's own lieutenant at Makapoo. So every man who could be spared at the larger infantry position, Mast among them, was sent to help unload the high explosive.

None of them from Makapoo had ever really seen the cave before. A four or five man detail of engineers under a young lieutenant had been placed there to guard it, although for what and from whom nobody knew, since the cave was totally empty except for its guards who when it rained wisely slept inside. So, not having been allowed inside it before, it was a treat to the men from Makapoo to get inside and look it over, even though the work of unloading was hard. For that matter, it was a treat to them to do anything: any detail, any job, any act: that would get them outside that encircling, isolating wall of wire which they had built around themselves and which they had all come gradually to hate. So the cave was a double treat. That is, it was a treat to everyone but Mast who had seen his pistol on the hip of Corporal Winstock.

It was an exciting cave, going deep back into the mountain before it opened out into the magazine, its high vaulted ceiling echoing and at the same time muffling the sounds of the working men, reflecting back in the gloom the light from the engineers' electric lanterns, while weird gnomelike shadows formed and moved grotesquely on the walls as the carriers themselves moved, an insane, mad, comically ironic parody of everything they did. Looking at those shadows would make even an uneducated man wonder about the seriousness of human endeavors, and it had that effect on almost all of them. But Mast hardly saw it at all. He was far too busy thinking about his pistol, *his* pistol, hanging there on Winstock's hip, and what things he could do to go about getting it back.

The working party, consisting of fifteen men from the position plus the four or five engineers, moved back and forth trampingly, through the gloomy gallery between the bright sunlight and dust of the trucks outside and the lamplit magazine, two shuttling lines, one carrying the heavy cases, the other returning for a new load. By the end of the day, with a break for lunch, they had unloaded five truck loads of explosive and the stacks of cases in the magazine had grown steadily higher until the cave was nearly filled. Almost everyone had the same reaction, which was a mixture of awe and an expressed desire to be around, but not too close, if it was ever detonated. It would be quite a sight. Shortly before suppertime it was done, and then it was back inside that hated, hateful, self-constructed wall of wire, the gate of which the sentry closed and locked after them. The excursion was over.

During the course of the day Mast had garnered several gossips' comments upon the appearance of his pistol on Winstock's hip. Everybody knew about it, and the opinions ran all the way from the one that Winstock had bought it from Mast for an extraordinary sum, to the one that Winstock had won it from Mast for nothing by a single cut of the cards for the pistol against an even more fabulous sum. But it was clear that Winstock had told somebody, perhaps several, that he had bought it from Mast.

Mast himself neither confirmed nor denied any

of these opinions and merely grinned knowingly, although he was raging inside. He still had not figured out how he was going to go about getting it back, unless he actually assaulted Winstock physically, a thing which he of course could not do in front of anyone since it was a court-martial offense. Court-martial offense or not, he was prepared to do even that, if he could get Winstock off to himself, because Mast felt he no longer owed Winstock the respect due a noncom. Mast was very emphatic about that. Winstock had already negated that respect himself, Mast felt righteously, when he had lied and cheated and used his rank as a noncom to get hold of the pistol by underhanded means. Mast was shocked and indignant when he thought about a noncom doing such a thing: A man who was a corporal was supposed to set an example of probity and integrity and inspire trust as a leader of men. Mast knew that were he himself a noncom, he would never do such a monstrous thing. He would take his duties and responsibilities far too seriously to do so. So Mast felt no compunction about hitting such a noncom. And besides, Winstock was smaller than Mast.

That evening after supper Mast approached the number two hole where a group had formed around two men who had guitars. He had seen both Winstock and his other enemy O'Brien there. Outside of talking, the guitar music and the singing that went with it (always provided the guitar players felt in the mood to play, of course) were about the only recreation left to those men who were no longer financially solvent enough to play poker.

Mast had already noted at evening chow that something had happened between Winstock and O'Brien. Winstock was still wearing the pistol, and it took only a few minutes to see that neither of them was speaking to the other. Lately, and for about a week before Winstock had pulled his lying, cheating, dishonest trick, the two men had been very chummy. But now whenever one of them said anything to anyone, the other always carefully turned his back or happened to be looking another way.

It was not hard to figure out that their coldness had something to do with the pistol. Mast suspected, from the way they'd had their heads together talking all the time for days, that O'Brien may have been in part responsible for the plot as to how to get it away from him. Possibly O'Brien had been going to buy it from Winstock after he got it, or more likely, since O'Brien was reputedly broke, he was to be given it in return for some favor or other. Only now that Winstock had it he was keeping it for himself. It had to be something of this sort.

The guitar session broke up soon, because once it was dark no more smoking was allowed out in the open. It was this that Mast had been waiting for. When Winstock, laughing and talking and with Mast's pistol jouncing securely on his hip, left the group and went off up the hill toward his own home hole the number five hole, Mast waited a few seconds and then got up and followed him, aware of O'Brien's pale green eyes, following *him*. He might not be able to whip O'Brien, but he was sure he could beat up Winstock.

"Winstock!" he called, climbing after him.

Other men were leaving the group too, spreading off toward their home holes or to get their blankets and go wherever it was they slept, some going down and some of them coming up this way through the deepening red dusk. So while Mast and Winstock were out of earshot they still were not strictly alone and out of sight. Mast made a mental note of this. Here would not be the place to fight him, where the court-martial offense could be seen.

"Well! Hello, Mast," Corporal Winstock said in a friendly way. He was standing a little above Mast, up the hill, on an outcropping. "Ain't seen you around in quite a spell. Not since they bust up our little detail, in fack."

Mast simply stood, staring at him unbelievingly. Such lack of guilt seemed impossible.

"Well, what can I do for you, Mast?" Winstock said cheerfully. "Did you want somethin'?"

"What can you do for me? I want my pistol back. That's what you can do for me."

"You want *what?*" Winstock said, his eyebrows going up.

"I said I want my pistol back. And I want it back right now."

"I don't know what you're talkin' about," Winstock said cheerfully. Through the deepening, almost blood-red dusk that was now nearly full night, he stared at Mast narrowly with his narrow little face.

"You don't 'hunh?" Mast said grimly. "Do you deny that you took my pistol away from me—*on your authority as a corporal*—to turn in to the supply room?"

"What?" Winstock said cheerfully. "Oh, that. Sure. Sure I did. I told you I was sorry I had to do it. What more can I say? And why the hell should I deny it?"

"Do you deny that that pistol you're wearing right now is the same pistol you took away from me?"

"Why, hell yes! Hell yes I deny it!" Winstock said, looking both indignant and surprised. "Oh, I see what's bothering you. You think this here pistol is the same one I taken off of you, and that I kep' it instead of turning it in like I said." He shook his head somberly. "That's a hell of a thing to accuse a man of, Mast, that's all."

"It just happens that I happen to know the serial number of that pistol I had," Mast said, boring on grimly. "I memorized it. Do you want to let me look at this pistol and check its serial number?"

Shocked indignation flashed over Winstock's

face. "Why, hell no! Who the hell are you? To be checkin' on me? You got no authority over me. You'll just have to take my word for it that this ain't your pistol, Mast."

"Then where did you get it?" Mast demanded.

"It's none of your business where I got it," Winstock said, calm and cheerful once again. "But for your information, I bought it."

"Bought it!" Mast jeered. "Where could you buy a pistol locked up on this beach position?"

"I bought it today off one of them engineer guys across the road."

"How could you buy it today when I saw it on you bright and early this morning?"

"I bought it yesterday," Winstock said unflinchingly.

Mast paused. He knew he was right, it was his pistol, he *knew* it, but from somewhere an element of doubt, a thought that Winstock might be telling the truth, might actually have turned Mast's pistol in and bought this other one from an engineer, had seeped into his mind. Winstock *looked* so truthful. It emasculated Mast's righteousness. And the element of doubt increased his already percipitate desperation.

"I could punch you in the head, Winstock," he said recklessly; "and take it away from you and see the serial number for myself."

"That's a court-martial offense," Winstock said immediately. "You'd be a fool to do it." He looked around through the swiftly falling night and nodded. "All these guys around to see it."

"I can wait till I get you by yourself."

"Ha!" Winstock laughed, throwing back his head. "How you gonna ever get *any*body by themself on this damn beach position? There's only four hundred yards of it."

Salvation! Salvation! Be saved! To be saved! The hope of survival! These words were running themselves over and over through Mast's mind, a sort of documentary commentary in a professional announcer's voice to his private movie of the Jap officer severing his body, as he stared at the man who had taken this salvation from him. For a desperate moment he thought of telling him the truth about how he had come into possession of the pistol, that there was a record of it after all. Then he thought of Musso's endorsing visit, which proved the pistol his, and once again the face of the man from the 8th Field, from whom he had not bought it, rose up in his mind's eye to confirm. He couldn't tell him. To do that would be to lose the pistol forever.

"Look, Winstock," he said flippantly. "I want to ask you something. Just for the record. Between us two. How can you equate—"

"Equate?" Winstock asked.

"Equalize. How can you equalize to yourself, in your own mind, the fact that you took my pistol away from me because I had bought it off a guy, and went and turned it in; and then turned right around and went and bought one yourself? How can you explain that? I'd just like to know."

"Well," Winstock said calmly, "it's easy. I just changed my mind, that's all. After I took yours. I'm just sorry that I went and turned yours in before I changed my mind. It's tough on you."

"Yeah," Mast said. "Sure is. A good answer," he said bitterly; "a fine answer."

"Look, Mast," Winstock said reasonably, and rested the heel of his palm possessively upon the object in question at his hip. "I want to explain somethin' to you. It's simple, and you should of saw it. With your education. But since you didn't, I'll explain it to you.

"How can you have a pistol? There ain't no record of you ever havin' no pistol. So how can you have one? You just never had a pistol. Don't you see?

"Now this pistol here," he wiggled his fingers without moving his palm from it, "is mine. I bought it, and it don't have nothin' to do with you at all. Besides, I need a pistol worse than you do. Or almost anybody. I'm a noncom. I'm second in command of a squad. I got people I got to look after. And who I got responsibilities to. That's why I need a pistol. What would happen to all those other people if somethin' happened to me? If the government knew what it was doin' it would of issued me a pistol. Hell, we get in combat, the squad leader'll probly be gone most of the time, if he ain't killed already, and then I'll have the whole squad to look after. Right?

"And you know what that is, Mast. When you're in command of a squad—or even second-in-command—you're a target. That's who those Jap officers with them Samurai sabers always go for first: the squad leader or assistant squad leader. You know that.

"This pistol," Winstock said contentedly, drumming his fingers against the leather of the holster flap for Mast's benefit without moving his palm from it, "this pistol might actually save my life someday, save *me*. You realize that? A pistol's the best defense there is against those wacky sabers. I wouldn't mind bein' shot so much.

"Now do you see why I need this pistol more than you? Hell, time we get in combat, you'll probly be workin' in the orderly room anyway, Mast. With your education. So if you even did have a pistol once, which you didn't, what would you need it for? Right?"

"I have no intention of ever working in the orderly room," Mast said desperately.

"I don't see how you can help it, Mast," Winstock said emphatically, giving his head a slow shake. "With your education. Now go on home and leave me be and stop this crap. Right? I'm just sorry that I turned that pistol of yours in before I got mine and changed my mind, that's all. But there's nothin' I can do about it for you now." He nodded once, emphatically, and started off on up the hill, the heel of his palm still resting possessively on the pistol butt.

Mast stood quietly, although internally he was seething with desperation, looking after him, aware that his cause was hopeless and that Winstock was right. He could never prove he'd had the pistol. And if he could, what then? Who would he prove it *to*? And Winstock was also right about catching him alone and taking it from him by force: it would be impossible within the narrow confines of this beach position. Mast turned and started back down the hill toward where he kept his blankets beneath a rock outcropping. Strangely, neither of them this time had even mentioned the possibility of going to Sergeant Pender and turning the pistol in, as he and O'Brien had threatened each other. Both of them knew better. Obviously there was only one thing left to do. If he wanted his pistol back at all, ever, there was only one way left to get it. He would have to steal it back. As he passed by the number two hole, O'Brien was still waiting there and Mast as he went on was aware of those pale green eyes following him searchingly and in silence. O'Brien of course could see he wasn't wearing it.

Once he had made up his mind to steal it back, Mast went about it thoroughly and intelligently. But he had some trouble in making up his mind. It was not a moral problem so much. It was the fact that he had to face and accept the possibility of the shame and public embarrassment of being caught. But in this case he had no other recourse. His first act, once he had made up his mind, was to go down into the number five hole, Winstock's home hole, at four in the morning when he got off post and 'case the joint,' as it were. The two men on post at the guns were sitting staring blindly in the dark out through the apertures from which protruded the snub noses of the two .30-caliber watercooled, talking quietly to each other to keep awake. Mast chatted with them while he took in the rest of the place.

Corporal Winstock himself was sleeping, rolled up right next to the door on the right as you entered. There were four other sleepers scattered about the raw rock floor. Winstock's head was toward the doorway at the foot of the steps cut into the solid rock, but he did not stir when Mast came in. His feet were toward the corner where in the gloom, lying right out in the open on top of a barracks bag which was apparently his, there was a rifle belt with a holstered pistol attached to it. Such fantastic luck was more than Mast had bargained for, and it partially unnerved him.

Among other things Mast noted that both men on post never turned around or took their eyes off the invisible night-black sea, even when they talked. It would have been easy just to pick up belt, holster, pistol and all and walk out with it, as far as those two were concerned. But Mast had come unprepared for such an easy-to-manage eventuality, he had prepared himself only for looking the place over. And he could not bring himself to make the fatal, conclusive movement of reaching out his arm. After chatting with them a while he got up and left.

Down below on the flat, where other men were sleeping out in the open in the wind as he did, Mast rolled up on the rocky ground and putting his shelterhalf over his head, smoked a cigarette. He should have done it while he was there, and what he ought to do now was go right back up there and get it. Winstock might not leave it out like that again. It was unbelievable that he had this time. Perhaps he didn't know about the nocturnal attempts to steal it. Mast had never told anyone. But it took a while for him to steel himself to it. After a second cigarette, which he carefully stubbed out on the ground beside the first before uncovering his head, Mast unwrapped himself and started back up the hill.

It was ridiculously easy. One of the things that had bothered Mast was the problem of taking Winstock's rifle belt. One of the least stolen items in the service, everyone nonetheless had his name and serial number inked or stamped on the inside of his rifle belt. To take it also would be to invoke the question of truly stolen equipment, something the taking of the pistol would not do. Mast might throw it away, over the cliff, but the problem of stolen equipment would still exist, something Winstock could legitimately use, perhaps against Mast himself.

He solved it easily, and simply. He simply went down into the hole, mumbled something about being unable to sleep, a statement never in question around this rocky, windy, uncomfortable place, and then while he talked to the two sleepy men who talked back but nevertheless did not look around, proceeded to unhook the holstered pistol from Winstock's belt, leaving the belt there, and attached it to his own. The magnitude of his own courage astounded him, as did the simple easiness of it. After putting his own belt back around his waist with the pistol on it, he removed the extra pistol clips from the pouch in Winstock's belt and put them in his own. Then he said good night and went back down and rolled up again, his pistol at his hip again. It was that easy. And as he buttoned his shirt down over it in his waist belt and zippered up his field jacket, the feeling of comfort that it gave him, being there again, was indescribable. Mast felt saved again, had a chance to survive again. And to hell with Corporal Winstock. When he checked the serial number, as the still-unresolved element of doubt forced him to do, although he did not want to, he found that it was really his own pistol.

Next day when he saw Winstock, the little corporal looked at him hatefully but there was nevertheless in his glance, despite the hate, a measure of respect that had never been in his eyes before when he looked at Mast. Apparently Winstock had ascertained for himself just what had happened last night. Mast did not say anything to him, and he did not say anything to Mast. And in fact, after that, Mast and Winstock did not speak at all, except when necessary in line of duty, just as Mast and O'Brien did not speak. But O'Brien, while he and Mast still did not speak, nevertheless appeared to be pleased that Winstock had not gotten away with his double swindle of both himself and Mast.

When two or three men, following the evolutions of the pistol about the beach position with the interest of uninvolved observers, asked him about having it back, Mast merely said he had changed his mind and bought it back from Winstock.

If Winstock objected to this explanation, Mast did not hear of it.

CHAPTER SEVEN

The loading of the demolition across the road caused a number of unanticipated changes in the lives of everyone at Makapoo. These changes were not immediately apparent, but they became increasingly clear as the days, and then the weeks, passed. Almost all of them were changes for the better.

The first change, which affected everybody on the position, and which also affected Mast and Mast's pistol, occurred a little over a week after Mast stole his pistol back from Winstock. This was the creation of a permanent five-man detail from the beach position to serve as a roadguard for the now-loaded demolition.

The story behind the creation of this roadguard was a complex one. But it can be explained easily with that phrase which has always done such excellent service in all the armies of the world: 'Somebody' screwed up. 'Somebody' forgot. And no one, of course, was able to figure out just who this 'Somebody' might be.

Now that the demolition was loaded, and thus became a physical fact, to be dealt with as such, it was discovered that it had not been provided with adequate protection for such an important, and potentially dangerous, installation. In the planning and correlation of the overall defense plan the planners somehow had neglected to provide the men, the guns, or the built-in positions for both, to protect the Makapuu Head demolition. And as a result, when the beach positions and other installations were constructed in October and November, none were constructed for it. Too late it was found that a theoretical enemy patrol in force, marching overland at night from an established beachhead somewhere along the twenty miles of beach in the Kaneohe Valley (which beachhead no one expected the Japanese not to accomplish) could simply come out of the foothills and walk right up the road and capture the demolition easily. All the pillboxes at Makapoo faced out to sea. Men coming up out of them to face this force at their rear would be slaughtered. The five engineers could not be expected to handle such a force. There was, in fact, around this very important and very dangerous strategic demolition nothing but a large hole for the enemy to plunge into. It was to alleviate this tactical blunder that the five-man roadguard from the Makapoo infantry position was created a week after the demolition had been loaded.

Probably, although it must naturally affect the life of the position, this new added element at Makapoo would not have affected Mast or his pistol. But as it turned out it was Mast's own squad leader who was put in charge of the roadguard by the young lieutenant. He was put in charge, and told to pick his own men, who because it was a suicide mission had to be volunteers. And so it was that one afternoon when Mast was off post and sitting on a rock in the sun because there was no work to do, his squad leader came around to him with a proposition, one which involved his new command, the roadguard.

Everyone at Makapoo knew all about the roadguard, naturally. Soldiers like to study with a professional eye and speculate over their own official dispositions which so vitally concern their very lives, whether they can do anything about them or not. So at Makapoo the men understood everything about the roadguard, about the tactical blunder which had occasioned it and for which it was a coverup, and about the new tactics which when inaugurated would make of the roadguard a veritable death trap suicide mission. The five men, one of them a BAR man, would be stationed at all times at the culvert at the foot of the rise where the road curved down the cliff. And should a landing ever be effected their job would be to hold off any patrols until the demolition could be blown behind them. After that they would be on their own and could try to get back to their unit as best they could. Everybody knew what that meant. That was why it was called a suicide mission, and why the men on it had to be volunteers.

Oddly enough, knowing all of this, every man at Makapoo wanted to volunteer for the roadguard and it was considered an enviable assignment. The reason was not hard to find. Apart from the fact that the roadguard allowed them to live outside the hated wall of wire, all the trucks and cars that went to market in the city used this highway. And in addition to their unpleasant duties with future Japanese patrols, they also had orders to stop and search all vehicles which used the road, for evidences of sabotage. Almost immediately, once the roadguard began operating, fresh fruit, bananas, candy bars, bottles of Coca-Cola and Seven-Up, even that rare, precious fifth of whiskey now and then, began to make their appearance within the position's isolating ring of wire. But if the position as a whole benefited in a small measure, the five men on the roadguard itself lived like kings. And for the first time since the war began, the Makapoo personnel—five of them, at any rate—were able to enjoy that new, lavish, civilian love of soldiery and get themselves adopted, as all the unisolated beach positions had done long ago with nearby homes. Almost at once each of the five chose, or was chosen by, his favorite daily produce trucker who brought him little things from home, in addition to the samples of his produce. Perhaps even more important they, the five, could talk to *people,* as distinguished from soldiers. Almost unlimited people. And some of them were females. Talking to females was better than nothing, although it made the grinding hunger stronger afterwards. There was not a single man below the first three grades at Makapoo who was not willing to risk the far-off future of potential Jap patrols, in order to partake of these small, but to them luxurious, benefits of now.

It was as the envied commander of this small but exclusive group of luxurious livers that Mast's squad leader came around to Mast with his proposition. Tall, quiet, sensitive—and intelligent, although he did not get further than first year high school in his native New England town— Buck-sergeant Thomas Burton was a good squad leader. He came up to where Mast was sitting on his rock outcropping, put his foot up on the rock, and leaned on his long leg looking hesitant and embarrassed.

"Want to talk to you."

Mast, immediately suspicious, looked back at Burton's level gaze with narrowed eye.

"Yeah? What about?"

Mast had not forgotten how Winstock, another noncom had trapped him when he was sitting just like this, alone.

"About that pistol of yours," Burton said.

He got no further. Mast got up immediately and started off without a word, toward people.

"Hey! Wait a minute!" Burton protested. "Come back here."

Mast stopped and turned to look back at him nervously. How did one protect oneself against noncoms, who could order one to do things?

"My pistol hasn't got anything to do with you. What do you want to know about my pistol?"

"Take it easy, take it easy. Come on back here," Burton said soothingly. Carefully, he did not move.

Still Mast hesitated.

"Look, I know all about what Winstock tried to pull on you," Burton said. "Anybody with an ounce of head could see he conned you into turnin' your pistol over to him to turn in, and then kept it himself. I wouldn't pull anything like that on you, Mast. Hell, you know that."

"How did you find out about that?" Mast said sullenly, refusing to look at him.

"I figured it out," Burton said. "That's all." He took his foot down from the rock slowly as if he were in the presence of a frightened wild creature. "You stole it back from him that night, didn't you?"

"Yeah," Mast said reluctantly.

"I figured. Pretty smart. Took a lot of guts too."

"What do you want?" Mast said abruptly, unflattered.

"Come on back here and sit down."

"No."

"Come on. I just want to talk to you. I got a proposition to make you," Burton said. "That's all. About your pistol."

"I don't want any propositions about my pistol," Mast said. It was almost a wail. "I don't want any propositions about anything. I just want to be left alone. I just want me and my pistol to be left alone together."

"I wouldn't try to beat you out of your pistol," Burton said, "come on back here. Look, did I ever say a word to you about your pistol? I've known about your pistol ever since we first hit this crummy position, haven't I? And did I ever try to make you turn it in or anything like that? I never said a word to you about it, did I?"

"No, that's true," Mast said reluctantly.

"Then come on back here and sit down, damn it," Burton said. "It won't hurt you any to listen to me. Won't hurt you to talk about it."

"But I don't want to talk about it," Mast said, but he came back toward the rock. "I don't even want to *think* about it. Everybody gets on me about my pistol. Everybody tries to steal it off me, or beat me out of it, or everything. I don't want to talk about it, or think about it, or fight about it, or anything else. I just want to be left alone with it. Is that too much to ask? Is it?"

"Sit down," Burton said.

Mast did.

"Now don't say anything. Just listen to me," Burton said. "Don't talk, just listen. That's all you have to do. That won't hurt you any. Okay?"

"Okay," Mast said.

"Okay. Now look. Here's my proposition," Burton said. He hesitated and the embarrassed look came back over his face. "See, I've made a lot of money at poker the last few days," he said by way of explanation, and then plunged on: "Here's my offer. I'll give you a hundred and fifty dollars cash. And I'll put you on the roadguard."

"For my pistol?"

"What else? Sure for your pistol."

Mast listened, but the words no longer had much meaning before this munificence. "On the roadguard?" he said vapidly.

"Sure. I can do it. All I have to do is tell the lieutenant one of the guys ain't doin' right and ask to have him relieved. Put you in his place."

"Well . . ." Mast said idiotically. It was a tremendous offer. A hundred and fifty dollars was almost five months pay for a private 1st class. "But, on the other hand," Mast blurted, answering himself aloud, "what good is money? There's no place to spend it except playing poker. I'd probably lose it all back in a week."

"Save it," Burton said. "Very likely they'll start giving us passes again in a month or two. Then you'll have it to take to town with you."

"Yes, but on the other hand, they might *not* give us passes."

"Okay, maybe they mightn't. But being on that roadguard is nothing to turn your nose up at, believe me."

"Yeah. I know that. Everybody wants on it," Mast said thoughtfully. "But why," he said after a moment; "why didn't you make me this offer before? when it first started? Instead of waiting till now?"

Again the look of hesitant embarrassment passed over Burton's face. He shrugged. "I had various favors to pay off to different guys," he said shortly.

"Well, but is that fair?" Mast said. "To kick a guy off, after you've put him on?"

"Why not? The favor's paid. I put him on."

"How do I know you wouldn't do the same thing to me?"

"Look. Let's get something straight. Let me explain something to you," Burton said urgently. "I would never kick somebody off the roadguard just to do myself a favor and get something I wanted. The guy I'm kickin' off needs to be kicked off. He's not been doing his work right, and he's been messing around too much. I see no reason why I shouldn't do myself a good turn too, though, as long as I'm doing my job right. The same holds true for you. If you didn't do your work well, I'd kick you off too. But if you did, you'd stay." Nevertheless, in spite of the extreme logic of his statement, there was still that faint look of embarrassment on his face, which Mast could sense, as if Burton hadn't quite convinced himself.

"Why does everybody want my pistol?" Mast said, almost plaintively.

"Well, why do you want it yourself?" Burton said.

"I don't really know. I guess it's because of those Samurai sabers. I got a hunch—a very strong hunch—it might save me from one of them someday. And I want to be saved. I guess it makes me feel more comfortable."

"Well, you can pretty nearly bet the others feel like you do," Burton said. "That's always a safe bet, I've found. You notice the Topkicker has one, in addition to his rifle. So does old Sergeant Pender."

"Sergeant Pender's had his since the first World War."

Doesn't matter. He's got it. And so does everybody else who can get themselves hold of one. I see no reason why I shouldn't have one too, if I can get one. You know yourself, Mast, that it's always the squad leaders and the officers that those Jap officers head for. We're more of a target than you privates. I could give you a lot of yak about me having responsibilities to my men and all that guff, and it wouldn't be entirely untrue either. But it ain't really the main point. The main point's that I want to be saved out of this war just as you or anybody."

"And so you want to buy my chance of being saved away from me."

"Sure, if I can. And don't forget, I'm offering

you a higher price than anybody else around here could."

"Yeah, okay. And then what'll happen to me when we get into combat?"

"Hell, Mast, this outfit may never get into combat. We may sit the whole war out guardin' this island. And it's damned unlikely the Japs will ever try to invade it now. And if that happens, if we do stay here, well, I'm just out and you're ahead, that's all. I'm just gambling with you, that's the size of it."

"Some gamble," Mast said unhappily.

"If the outfit did go into combat, there's no reason why you should have to. With your education," Burton said. "Being a high school graduate and all, you could go into the orderly room or get yourself a good desk job, even, in personnel or someplace else in the Rear Echelon. Any time you wanted."

"Yeah, everybody tells me that. Everybody that wants my pistol, anyway. I don't want a job in the Rear Echelon. I'm not yellow."

"But maybe you'd be helping the war effort better if you did."

"To hell with the war effort. I'm not yellow. I may be scared, but I'm not a coward."

"Well, that's up to you," Burton said. "I think you're silly. Not to take advantage of a safe deal like that.

"Anyway, just don't sell my roadguard short. It's a hell of a good deal. Hell, we're even cookin' our own meals down there now. We get hamburger every day off those people. Steak, every other day. And we've always got some whiskey around. Don't think my roadguard ain't a good deal."

"Yeah, I know that," Mast said unhappily.

"Take some time to think about it," Burton said. "Don't make up your mind right now. I know it's a tough decision. I'll come back later." He got up off the rock outcropping where they had both been sitting, nodded brusquely, and started off. But after he had gone a few yards, he stopped and turned back.

"Don't think I didn't think a long time about it before deciding to make you an offer like this. But I don't think it's bad or dishonorable. Otherwise I wouldn't do it."

There was a look almost of appeal in Burton's level gaze, but Mast was too immersed in his own unhappiness to respond more than feebly.

"Yeah. I guess so, too. Well, I'll let you know."

Without answering again, as though he knew it to be useless, both for his appeal and for an answer, now, to his proposition, Burton turned and started on. Mast watched him go, thinking angrily that Burton had no right to force a decision like this on him. Lately, since he had got it back from Winstock, thought of his pistol and his awareness of his responsibility to it occupied more and more of his time, attention, and his energy. There was almost nothing he did or said now that was not at least partially concerned with the pistol and how to protect it. And now this was being forced upon him, too.

Because he was angry, Mast was able to believe his opinion of Burton had undergone a considerable lowering, and he clutched this idea to him gratefully to strengthen his indignation and resolve. His own squad leader, whom he had looked up to and respected! Even if he hadn't used force or coercion, Burton nonetheless was guilty of a grave moral infraction in using his rank for personal gain. And Mast did not intend to absolve him, whether he ever spoke of it to him or not.

On the other hand, there was the roadguard, enticing him, just waiting there for him. And Mast would have loved dearly to be on it. In the end it was his strong moral resolve not to be party to any such act as Burton had suggested, not to be responsible for getting some poor guy who didn't deserve it kicked off the roadguard, that sustained him.

He told Burton his decision the next day at noon chow, and the Sergeant only listened and then nodded in silence.

"I suppose there's no chance of my getting on the roadguard any other way?" Mast asked.

"Nope," Burton said. "I told you. When I relieve anyone I'll make damned sure it won't be you who'll replace him. But if you ever change your mind, the offer still stands. I've put the hundred and fifty away and I don't intend to spend or lose it. I want that pistol damn bad. So just remember, the offer's still there if you ever want it."

And so Mast had a new thing to live with, one that certainly did not make his life any the more pleasant. Day by day, unhappily, Mast went about his various jobs with the knowledge that he could be on the roadguard living in comparative luxury, any time he wanted to change his mind and sell the pistol.

CHAPTER EIGHT

In a way, ironically enough, it was Burton's refusal to accept Mast on the roadguard on any other terms than surrender of his pistol which was responsible for what was probably the most pleasant experience Mast had during his whole time in Hawaii. At least, it was pleasant for most of its time. Because it too endangered Mast's pistol, momentarily.

A few weeks after the inauguration of the roadguard, the strategy-planners of the Hawaiian Department discovered—or at least decided to cope with—another loophole in their network of defenses along the Koolau Range which ended in the cliff at Makapuu. This was a little-known and very difficult pass through the mountains a few miles inland known as Marconi Pass. Actually it was a little more than a low place, a slight saddle, in the main ridge; but due to rockfalls and the accumulation of detritus it was possible to climb it from the steeper Kaneohe side. In 1940 a picked squad of infantry had proved this without casualty or injury, as a tactical exercise. This Marconi Pass being the only possible point of crossing between Makapuu and the celebrated Pali, at which point the range turned north and became less dangerous to the city, it was decided to put a permanent four-man patrol up there with two machine guns; two MGs and a few cases of grenades, it was believed, could handle any number of enemy troops attempting to make the climb. Mast's company was picked to provide the men because its sector of beach was nearest to the pass, and for logistic reasons of his own the company commander chose to send the men from the Makapoo position. Mast was one of them.

Old Makapoo, so familiar in all its discomforts now to everyone, had changed considerably in the weeks since the origination of the roadguard. After a personal inspection by high officers of the staff, it had been decided that the position was undermanned and orders were sent down to the commander of Mast's company to increase the complement by half a platoon. These two squads, the orders said, were to come from the company reserve at Hanauma Bay. So Makapuu Head was at least a little bit rejuvenated, by an influx of two squads of deeply disgruntled men who did not at all enjoy leaving the quiet peace and swimming of the command post for the storm and wind and tentless rocks of Makapoo. It was, in actual fact, good for the position, but all Mast himself could see through depressed eyes was the arrival of nineteen more men (all squads were understrength) who would want to relieve him of his pistol.

But in addition to this and, to the men on the position at least, of more importance, the company commander had seized the opportunity of the inspection to point out to the inspecting brass the conditions under which his men had been living for the past two months. As a result, after a couple of weeks, as though reluctantly, trucks began to arrive from time to time with stacks of two-by-fours, or stacks of raw pine tongue-and-groove, kegs of nails, bags of cement, paper, tar, and hammers. Mast, along with a large number of others, suddenly found himself engaged in learning by practice the trade of carpenter. There were, it turned out, to everyone's surprise, several former professional carpenters at Makapoo, masquerading in the guise of infantrymen. And old Sergeant Pender, at one time or other in his twenty-eight years in the Army, had learned this trade along with a dozen others. Under his direction the former carpenters were put in charge, and the men at Makapoo began to build for themselves the shelter nobody else had found the time to build for them. By the time the orders concerning the Marconi Pass patrol arrived, the concrete-in-nailkeg foundations were laid, the beams and joists were laid, the studding was up, most of the rafters were set, and the siding was beginning to go on.

Sergeant Pender, slyly shunted the responsibility of picking the patrol by the young lieutenant who came down from the field phone with the orders, stepped outside the doorway of the hutment he was working on, took the nails out of his mouth, wiped his grizzled head while he thought, then bellowed for Burton's assistant squad leader, Corporal Fondriere. With Burton detached to the roadguard Burton's squad was already split anyway. Then he bawled the names of his three most inept students of carpentry, a great deal of which work still lay ahead of all of them, put the nails back in his mouth and went back to work. One of them was Mast. Another was O'Brien. The third was a tall thin southerner named Grace. Thus was the historical first Marconi Pass patrol chosen.

A two-and-a-half-ton truck picked them up, and they reported in to the first sergeant at the CP with all their gear. The company commander himself, whom even back in peacetime they saw to speak to only about once in three months unless it was by their own request, explained their duties to them and showed them himself on the map where they would be and the strategic and tactical reasons for it. Everything was being prepared for them that they'd need, he said. All they had to do, now, was wait for it. The company commander could not tell them exactly how long they would be up there, but he judged it would be about a week or ten days before they were relieved. (Actually, as it turned out, it was more than two weeks and they were almost out of food; but nobody minded.) The company commander went on to say that he had asked for picked men, so he knew they knew their business. He would not try to give them a peptalk except to say that they would be up there entirely on their own, with no higher authority anywhere, that the eyes of the Hawaiian Department would be upon them, and that he trusted them. He was sorry, he smiled kindly, but he really did have to get back to work. After that they strolled lazily around the grove of thorn trees, walked out to the little bluff and leaned on the fence and looked at the sea, and concentrated on buying up all the candy bars they could get hold of from the CP personnel, who were able to send money in with the kitchen truck which served the other half of the company sector, the town half. They were unable to find any whiskey. All four of them felt a great sense of warmth for the company commander. They thought it nice of him to take so much of his valuable time with them. They wanted to do a good job for him. It was not that there was not any whiskey here, at the CP, they all knew that, it was just that no one would part with it for mere money.

Soldiers have a great instinct for being suspicious of kindnesses. Any time things are made easy for them, they are wary. But they also know that since they have no choice anyway, they might as well take advantage of whatever little benefits are offered them. So it was with the historic first Marconi Pass patrol. While a detail sweated and cursed loading their supplies they were to take with them, the patrol itself loafed and drank coffee and basked in its newfound notoriety. The cooks even went so far as to make up special hot sandwiches for them even though it wasn't mealtime. And at one time or another almost everyone at the CP came around to discuss their assignment with them. But all too soon, as they had known it would, this flattering attention and extra service ended and the truth began, and they were gone, off out on the highway in the truck with no more audiences.

They were being guided by a Signal Corps Pfc who was one of the few men in the Hawaiian Department to have scouted this area. He had been found especially for this mission. He rode up in the cab with the driver. The four of them rode in the back. And the floor of the truckbed was so crammed with their supplies that they were jammed all together at the very back. There were ten gallon milk cans of water, cases of C ration, boxes of other food such as eggs, canned beans and bacon supplied by the kitchen, axes, picks, Very pistols, ropes, as well as their two machine guns and case after case of ammunition and grenades. They were well supplied, and soon they found out how far they were going to have to carry it.

Leaving the CP the truck had turned east back toward Makapuu, but about halfway there it left the highway and turned inland, stopped for a wire gate which the Signal Corps Pfc got out and opened, and then ground on along a dirt road that was no more than two tracks through what appeared to be a cattle feeding ranch. Down on the flat, aged Hawaiians and Japanese who were apparently caretakers for the ranch peered at them from rickety little shacks from which cooking smoke drifted, but soon they began to rise and even these were left behind. Before long the tracks of the dirt road disappeared, and the truck ground on up through steepening open fields in which the trees and little fingers of forest became steadily more numerous, making its own road in and out among rock outcroppings which became thicker and thicker. Finally it reached a point where it could go no further, at the spot the Signal Corps Pfc had been looking for. This spot was the bottom of a steep, tree-grown, boulder-strewn, dry mountain runlet, too rocky and too steep even to be called a creekbed, at the point where it debouched into an honest, if steep, dry streambed. Here the truck stopped and they got out, and with the driver's help began to unload it.

High above them, up the tree-studded, rock-strewn chute which would be their staircase and appearing to be almost straight up, towered the main ridge of the Koolau Range. Below them out over the last clearing the truck had crossed they could see far, far below the highway, the beach and the sea. A car traveling along the highway appeared to be the size of a lighter flint and they watched it, fascinated, until it disappeared. Without exception the first Marconi Pass patrol had the feeling they were standing out in the open, protectionless, on the side of a steep roof, and the effect of the height gave them the optical illusion that they could just simply sit down and slide all the way back down to the highway. But it was when they turned the other way and looked up that their eyes widened and awe really took them.

"Are *we* going to carry all *this* up *there?*" someone said.

The Signal Corps Pfc, who wore a big sheath knife on his web pistol belt just behind his pistol and was apparently a member of some 'Pioneers' outfit or other, organized the unloading and the separation of the supplies into individual loads, and then prepared to leave.

"But aren't you going to help us carry this stuff up there?" Corporal Fondriere asked him.

"Hell no," the Signal Corps Pfc said. "You think I'm crazy?"

"But what if we get lost?"

"How can you get lost? There's nowhere else to go. Unless you were to cross one of these side ridges and leave this draw entirely. If you *could* cross one of these side ridges. You follow this—" he paused, searching for an appropriate word, then gave up and jerked his head at the tangled, dry, boulder-strewn giant's staircase, "—this *creek*bed up as far as it goes. Then you go straight on up about two hundred yards more, and there you are. It's the saddle between the two high points. You can't miss it."

He stared at them combatively for a moment, as if daring them even to try and miss it.

"I've been there. I've seen it. What the hell do I want to go back for? Anyway it'll take you three days to get this gear up there. See you in a week with your relief. Come on, Mack," he said to the driver.

So the historic first Marconi Pass patrol stood dumbly and watched truck, driver and guide disappear down the mountainside, leaving them in what suddenly and for the first time appeared to be this remarkably hostile mountain wilderness, now that they were alone.

"Well, let's get with it," Corporal Fondriere sighed.

It did not, after all, actually take them three days to get the gear up. It took them only two days, two whole days. It was nearly noon when the truck left them and they started the first climb, and it was nearly noon of the third day when the last case of grenades started its trip to the top. Corporal Fondriere, who never had been a forceful man and who had acquired his corporal's rank simply by staying in the Army nine years, decided that they would take the milk cans of water up first. There were four of these. They started off with all four, one to each man. At the first huge boulder they had to climb up around, two cans had to be left behind, and they were down to one can to each two men. Farther up, about three-quarters of the way to the top, where the mountain runlet became an actual rock chimney just before it came out onto the open slope, the third can was left precariously perched on a relatively level boulder, and they were down to four men to one can. Even so, they very nearly didn't make it.

Luckily, there were enough cracks and small ledges in the chimney so that they could rest the edge of the can on something whenever one or the other man had to move up to a new foothold. But when they came out breathing heavily onto the open slope, thinking their worst troubles were over, they discovered first that this slope which had appeared as such a haven from below was one of fifty or sixty degrees; and second they discovered that there was nothing up here, absolutely nothing, to hold onto except grass, which pulled out. The trees had stopped near the bottom of the chimney. Up here, they felt that they were *really* out in the open on the side of a roof. And that was exactly what it was like.

The only way to surmount this new obstacle was to crawl, crablike, two men in front pulling and two behind shoving, and literally draw the milk can the last two hundred yards to the top. For every ten yards they gained someone would start to slip back, and the only way to stop was to roll over and dig your heels in under you. The only way to rest was to dig a dirt ledge with the shoeheels and set the can upright and squat around it, because to let go of the can at all would be to lose it entirely.

At the very top, in the saddle itself, the slope lessened considerably until it was no more than twenty degrees, before it plunged itself abruptly over the other side into sheer rock. They left the fourth can there and went cautiously back down after the third can at the bottom of the chimney, and brought it up. Then they went all the way, almost to the bottom, for the other two cans, and repeated the first two climbs. All of the other gear, the cases and boxes and the machine guns and their tripods, was brought up in the same way, in stages, but nothing that they had to carry was as awkward and dangerous and nearly impossible to handle as those first four round milk cans of water. On every trip, all the way up to the chimney, tree roots and branches caught at them throwing them off balance on the slippery rocks, and when they got above there where they could have used them, they ceased. It was as if the mountain itself had a personal enmity for them. They worked all that afternoon until dark, and worked all the entire next day, and worked the entire morning of the following day.

It was bruising, grueling, killing work. But if the work was killing, it was nevertheless forgotten and made to count as nothing by what they saw that very first time they came up into the saddle of the pass with that first milk can of water. And each time they climbed exhaustedly back up with some new piece of gear, the experience was repeated as if it had never happened, refreshing them. Each time it was as if they had not seen it before.

The view was literally breathtaking. The whole of the Kaneohe Valley lay spread out before them in all its patchwork, verdant floorplan, running on to the north between the mountains and the sea until it lost itself in the mists of distance, looking much the same (except for modernizations) as it must have looked to Kamehameha's men when they first climbed to the Pali. Standing up here in the unobstructed winds of the upper air, which made them acutely aware of the height, they had spread out for them at their feet in a way which gave them a peculiar feeling of proprietorship, almost a fifth of the entire island. From the white surf of the beaches which they could see to the east, to the cloud-draped mountains in the west, it was their personal possession because they stood above it. As they stood and watched that first time, a B-18 bomber took off from Bellows Field in the valley below and climbed to its chosen height and began to practice maneuvers. It was still over a thousand feet *below* them, and they stood and looked at it first with astonishment, and then with superiority.

To be here, to be the first men to be stationed here if not actually the first to be here, and to live here for a week or ten days, there were to all four of them more than worth the heartbreaking work of getting their supplies up. During their stay (actually it was seventeen days, before their relief arrived) they did not once set foot on level ground, and walking on slopes became so natural that they were surprised to find flat earth when they finally came down. The pass itself, its saddle funneling all the winds as it did, was far too turbulent to pitch their sheltertents in, or stay in, except for the one man who was supposed to stay on post at the guns. But after exploration they found another comparatively level slope around the corner of rock beside the saddle, and here they pitched their two puptents, rigged up a rock-lined firepit, and made their camp. Here they cooked, heated water with which to shave, washed themselves when they felt like it which was seldom, and lived. They slept always on a slant. But they had been smart enough in the beginning to pitch the little sheltertents so that they opened down the slope with the closed ends up, in order to have their heads above their feet. As a result they enjoyed the unique experience of crawling up into their beds every night. It was like a quiet cove, their little slope with its two small tents pitched on either side, the firepit and the cooking utensils and axes and other gear scattered around, out of the wind and the weather, and it quickly acquired a quality of home, of being lived in. Most of their days when they weren't on post they spent exploring like excited boys, singly or together, along the treeless slopes of the main ridge or down in the edges of the forest.

It was the first time since Mast's company had moved out for the beaches, and Mast himself had come into possession of the pistol, that Mast had been happy. And the reason, had Mast looked for it, which he did not, was easy to find. It was because up here he felt he no longer had to think about protecting the pistol.

The awareness of the state of war in which they lived, and which gave the pistol its meaning, had not left Mast. It had not left any of them—although in actual fact there were moments up here, especially when he was exploring, that Mast forgot about it. But most of the time this cloud (with which they all were to become so familiar over the next several years, until it became almost second nature to them) was there, fully sensed, in the back of his mind and looming over everything. So Mast's particular, personal enemy, his devil, the Japanese major with the saber, had not left Mast. He was still there. But he had been abstracted by this free mountain living from an actual flesh-and-blood picture in Mast's mind to a mere idea. And as with so many people, mere abstract ideas were not nearly as disturbing to Mast as immediate actualities.

Probably a great deal of Mast's relief from the tension caused by the need to protect his salvation, the pistol, came from the fact that up here on top of the mountains the constant, omnipresent, omnipotent authority of the Army over every tiniest facet of their lives was removed from them, pushed back to the middle distance. Up here that Authority was represented only by the unforceful, amiable command of Corporal Fondriere.

And apparently Fondriere felt something of this same thing because after the first few days Fondriere did not even insist that one man stay on post at the guns at all times. After all, as he said, from here they could see the beaches where the Japs would land. Time enough, when they landed, to have a full-time sentry. All he asked was that there be one man in the camp at all times. After that the whole thing became one big vacation.

Mast had been under tremendous strain at Makapoo, trying to protect the pistol, and knowing all the time that all around him were numbers of men just waiting for a chance to grab it. He hadn't been able to enjoy anything, even life itself, because of the pistol. And so now, when he let down and relaxed, he let down all the way. He stopped the uncomfortable business of wearing the pistol inside his waist belt under his shirt at night, stopped wearing to bed the rifle belt with the holster on it. He wrapped it all up in itself and left the whole thing to lie at his head in the closed end of the tent, and began to get his first good sleep in weeks. He even stopped wearing the rifle belt in the daytime, as the others had theirs, and left it in the tent. Who could be an efficient rock-climber with that thing dragging at your waist?

After all, as he reasoned, there were only the four of them up here. And they were living in such close proximity in their little camp that there was no possibility of hiding a theft. Then too, being up here as they were, with the world, the war, the Army, everything so remote, it seemed somehow as if some sort of truce existed, not only about the pistol but about everything, between the four of them. And they were all enjoying it. It would be a ghastly immorality for any one of them to violate this feeling, and apparently they all felt it. This was evidenced by O'Brien.

Mast's relationship with O'Brien had remained the same as at Makapoo: they spoke to each other only when absolutely necessary in some line of duty. But up here, whether it was this sense of having been removed from under the thumb of Army authority, or whether it was because of having shared the now unbelievable job of bringing up the supplies, or whether it was just simply the being thrown together so much on the patrol, the two of them had started speaking when it was *not* in line of duty. It started first with a few stiff, brusque "Hellos," each man looking at the other tentatively, ready to draw back if rebuffed. Later a few other stiff words were added, finally a grin or two. And then one day O'Brien came up to Mast where he was sitting alone in the pass looking out over the valley that none of them ever tired of viewing, and made a pronouncement:

"Look. I know you're leavin' your pistol in your tent. I just wanted to tell you you don't have to worry about me snitching it. Not while we're up here anyway."

Mast had already sensed this attitude, not only in O'Brien but in everyone, or so he thought; otherwise he would never have dared leave the pistol. But now that O'Brien spoke it aloud, he was somehow embarrassed and at a loss for anything to say. "Well, thanks, O'Brien."

O'Brien sat down stiffly and looked out over the valley floor for himself. It was dappled by moving cloud shadows today, and far off miles away one cloud, one single cloud, was raining. "It's different up here somehow. I don't know why. I guess it's because the war seems so far away maybe."

"I guess that's it," Mast said embarrassedly. Far below at Bellows Field a plane took off in the sunshine and began to circle upward, still far below them.

"It don't really seem like the Army up here," O'Brien said stiffly.

"No, it doesn't."

"But don't get me wrong, Mast. I still want that pistol. I think I got a better right to it than you do. And once we get back down below I'll get it off you hook or crook any way I can, see? You don't need it. I need it. Now if you want it that way and be friends up here, okay and if you don't, okay."

"All right, let's leave it like that then," Mast said stiffly.

"Okay," O'Brien said just as stiffly, and stuck out his big hamlike hand. "Our valley looks pretty today, don't it?" he said after a moment, after they had shaken.

"Yes, it sure does," Mast said. They had all four of them started calling it that: 'our valley': as a joke about the feeling of possession that looking down from up here gave them.

Suddenly, from nowhere and for no reason, at least for no reason that he himself could ascertain, a fit of some unnamable emotion seized Mast so strongly that he was afraid for a moment he might weep. Because of this he got up and abruptly walked away, filled with astonishment at himself.

Well, at least his pistol was safe for the rest of the time they were up here anyway, and he could rest. Or so he thought. The only trouble was that it wasn't; wasn't safe. On the tenth day of the sojourn in Marconi Pass the fourth man, the tall thin quiet southerner Grace, tried to steal it—or rather just simply take it.

CHAPTER NINE

Actually, if it was the withdrawal of Army authority which had been in large part responsible for Mast's newfound happiness, it was also this same absence of authority which was eventually responsible for endangering the pistol again.

Apparently the tall, thin, quiet, amiable southerner Grace, who had been Mast's bunkmate since they arrived, had stood as long as he could the prospect, and the temptation, of seeing Mast's unregistered pistol lying there unprotected at the head of their tent day in and day out. Finally he had succumbed. At any rate on the tenth day of their stay Mast came back to the camp from exploring a new rock pinnacle to catch Grace alone in camp and in the act of attaching the pistol to his own rifle belt, after having detached it from Mast's.

"Hey!" Mast cried in alarm. "Hey! What are you doing!"

The southerner looked up and grinned, a tough, evil grin not at all like the quiet amiable man with whom Mast had shared a tent the past ten days. "What does it look like, Mast?" he said.

Mast, still standing at the bend of the little trail that they had gradually trampled in where it rounded the corner of rock from the saddle, could hardly believe what his eyes were offering him. "But you can't!" he cried, disjointed words and bits and pieces of thoughts running through his head without coherence, not only about the pistol but about the meaning of the Pass itself and what O'Brien had said. "You can't! Not up here! Not at the Pass!"

Grace, who had already had one hook of the holster through its eyelet, stopped working with it and looked up with that tough, mean grin which Mast could not recognize as belonging to him. "What's to stop me?"

"We will!" Mast said. "All of us!"

"No you won't, Grace said, still holding the half-fastened holster and belt in his hands. Mast had started to walk toward him, but he did not move. "What have them two guys got to do with you and this pistol? You think they'll help you? They will not. And you ain't big enough, nor tough enough, to stop me.

"Look, Mast," he said as Mast continued to advance along the trail. "You say you bought this pistol. But how do I know you bought it? Maybe you stole it. Even if you did buy it, somebody else stole it, didn't they? All right, I'm stealing it. Or rather, just taking it."

Mast had continued to come on, and now stopped a few feet away from him. "But you can't. Don't you understand? Not up here at the Pass, anyway. Are you a human being? Don't you have any honor? Don't you have any honesty? or integrity?"

"Did you have any in-tegrity when you bought a pistol you knew was stolen property? I guess I got as much as the next man," Grace said with his tough, mean grin. "Look, Mast. This is our last day up here. The Company Commander said we'd be relieved in ten days, didn't he? All right. I waited till the last day to do it. I've liked it up here too. I didn't want to spoil it. So I waited. Because I didn't want to spoil it. But I'd be a damn fool to wait any longer. Our relief might show up any minute now. And when that happens, it's done.

"When we get down from here, everything starts right over where it left off. We're back in the Army again then and God knows where we'll be a week from now. As soon as you get down off this mountain, you'll start sleeping with this pistol inside your shirt again. And what chance'll I ever have to get hold of it then?"

"But that's cheating!" Mast said. "You knew I trusted everybody."

"What's cheating," Grace said indifferently. "It all depends on how you look at it. I don't look at it that it's cheating. Way I look at it, you've been cheating me. Because I need this pistol worse than you do.

"Look, Mast," he said, still holding it in his hands, it still only half-fastened, his tone sober and serious and intent. "You know what my spec number is on the T.O., don't you? I'm a runner. I'm one of three company runners. Message carrier. Who stands to get it worse than a company runner? I'll be off on my own all the time, alone, maybe even traveling through the Jap lines, for all I know. What if I run into a patrol, out there all by myself? with some wacky officer with one of them damn Samurai sabers in charge of it? What if I lost my rifle and got captured? At least this way I'll be able to maybe get me a couple of officers and have a bullet left for myself. You know how they torture their prisoners and cut them all up with those sabers."

Grace's voice was very intent now. "While look at you, on the other hand. You're a born clerk, Mast. With your education. You'll wind up working for the Rear Echelon as company clerk, sure as hell, before you're done. What good will this pistol do you there?"

"I have no intention of ever becoming a clerk," Mast said in a voice which it seemed to him had become ancient, merely from repeating so many times the same words.

"Maybe not, but you will," Grace said with conviction. "And I see no reason why you should have this pistol back there, when I need it so bad up front."

"Say what you wish," Mast said. "You're a thief. And a cheat and a sneak."

"I don't think so," Grace said. "In fact, I know so."

As they stood staring at each other, separated by this difference of opinion, Mast heard footfalls behind him on the trail and turned to see Fondriere and O'Brien coming in from some exploration. "Well, you won't get away with it!" he cried over his shoulder at Grace, and turning back and spreading out his arms in appeal, poured out to them the story of Grace's defection and of just what had happened.

Grace continued to stand behind him listening stolidly, still holding the half-fastened holster and belt in his hands.

Not only did Grace, who was his own bunkmate, Mast pointed out, abuse his trust. Not only did Grace conduct himself like a thief and throw away his own honor and integrity. He had done what was much worse: he had destroyed the trip, and the Pass, and the Valley, and all that these had meant to all of them, the peacefulness and serenity and rest and memories they had all of them had up here. Mast made quite an interesting little speech, in a very few seconds. "Are we going to let him get away with it?" he summed up, spreading his hands again.

Corporal Fondriere coughed embarrassedly and dropped his eyes, and O'Brien, his face setting itself into a sheepish mask of studied disinterest, looked away.

"Your pistol doesn't have anything to do with my command," Fondriere said, "or with my mission up here. I don't see what it has to do with me and O'Brien. Whoever has your pistol it's not going to do me a damn bit of good."

"That's true," O'Brien said. "I think it's between you and Grace. Your pistol don't do me any good. I don't think you even got any right to ask us."

Mast stared at them, his arms still outspread, unable to believe that they would not help him, just on moral grounds alone. Not even considering what he meant to them as a person. Flashes and smatterings of all kinds of thoughts and feelings tore through him, the ruined peacefulness of the Pass here, his own violated trustfulness, the precious rest he had had for ten days but which was now lost, the cheap reaction of the two men before him to what was clearly a deep moral issue, the unconscionable lack of integrity of the man behind him. Mast could not even have separated them one from the other, so vague were they and so fast through his mind did they fly, but the sum total of all of them was outraged righteousness.

Armed with this, he turned abruptly and ran full force at Grace, butting him in the chest with his head and making a grab for the half-fastened pistol holster at the same time. Grace was standing on the path just in front of the tents where the lesser slope of the camp dropped away to the steeper slope down to the rock chimney. The force of Mast's head striking him in the chest threw him off balance. Instinctively, he stepped back—and off the slope. The drop under his foot wasn't much, a foot or two. But it was enough to make him fall, and when he fell he let go of the belt and pistol. Mast stood on the path, breathing heavily and once again in possession of the pistol, and watched Grace rolling down the steep slope toward the cup of the rock chimney into which everything on three sides, up here, would roll and fall.

Grace rolled thirty or forty yards down the two hundred yards of slope before he was able to dig in his heels and get himself stopped. He got up and in a half-scrambling run, staring up and grinning that mean, tough, squint-eyed grin, more a leer now than a grin, started back up the slope at Mast.

Mast, watching him, hastily and nervously set about getting the holster off the belt. Luckily for him it was only half-fastened or he wouldn't have made it in time. He tossed the belt toward the tents behind him but continued to clutch the heavy, holstered pistol because he no longer trusted putting it down, and waited.

A few yards from the top Grace intelligently changed his direction off to the side, although it never would have occurred to Mast to kick him. Thus he came up to the path level with Mast eight or ten yards away. Pausing to breathe a moment and still wearing that fixed grin, he came down the path with his fists up. He was just about a head taller than Mast, although a little less husky, but his arms were at least six inches longer. Mast, trying to defend himself while still clutching the holstered pistol, took his first punch hard on the ear, making his whole head ring. It knocked him off of the path, and because he would not let go of the pistol he landed heavily on his side—and immediately found himself rolling dizzily down the slope toward the chimney, as Grace had done before him.

He still would not let go of the pistol, but by digging in the fingernails of his free hand and trying to dig in first with his toes and then his heels as he turned, he managed to squirm himself around perpendicular to the slope and get himself stopped.

Then he too started to scramble back up to the path. He knew now that to have possession of the pistol was not enough. He had to make Grace give it up voluntarily by whipping him, or Grace would make him. But he still couldn't put the pistol down anywhere for fear of O'Brien or Fondriere taking it. He attempted, as he came back up, to utilize the same tactic Grace had, by turning off to one side, now that he knew about the kicking. But Grace, who had thought it up first, was not to be caught that way. He ran down the path above Mast, keeping himself directly above him.

A few feet from the top, just beyond kicking range, Mast stopped, breathing heavily, still clutching the pistol in his left hand.

"Come on, damn you," Grace drawled. "I'm

ready. I'll kick your face off."

Obviously there was nothing for it but to go on up, and Mast gathered himself, still staring upward, still breathing heavily. It was then that O'Brien intervened.

"Wait a minute! Mast, give me the pistol and I'll hold it for you."

"You!" Mast breathed.

"I promise I won't keep it. I'll give it back to you. Or to Grace, if you say so. Hell, you can't fight like that."

"He'll say so," Grace said with his mean grin.

"You think so?" Mast said. "All right," he said to O'Brien. "Let me come on up," he added, directing it at Grace.

"Go to hell," Grace grinned. "I'm not giving away no advantages."

"Here," O'Brien said, and came down onto the path a few feet from Grace. "Toss it up then."

For a long moment Mast stared at him in silence, breathing heavily.

"I promise I'll give it back to you," O'Brien said. "Or to Grace, if you say. I ain't that kind of a louse. Not if I promise."

After a moment of thought, staring up at him, Mast tossed the holstered pistol up to him in silence, and prepared himself to rush Grace. There was no other way to do it.

Mast jerked his head sideways when he saw it coming, and the kick grazed his ear, the same ear that had taken the punch earlier, and a hot streak of fire ran along the whole side of his head. Hurting fearfully, he dove upward and got Grace's other leg with both hands and upended him, then rolled sideways and pulled. Grace, cursing savagely, tumbled on down over Mast's back and commenced to roll down the slope again until he could get himself stopped, and Mast was once again in command of the path.

This time when Grace charged him, he did not allow Grace to go to the side but stayed in front of him as Grace had done to him. Just beyond range, Grace stopped too, gathering himself and his courage, and also getting a little wind. Then he charged, grinning evilly, his eyes wide and piercing. Mast, who had once had a one-semester course in boxing in high school, feinted, shifting his weight to his left foot, and when Grace jerked his head aside, delivered him a vicious kick in the face which carried with it all the righteous outrage that had been smouldering in him since this thing had started, that had been smouldering in him since long before that even, since all the way back to when the first man had tried the first time to beat him out of his pistol and his chance of being saved. And it was that kick that eventually won him the fight.

With a yelp of pain and then a stream of cursing Grace went over backwards with both hands to his face. When he finally got himself stopped on the slope, he paused crouching, his right hand to the already swelling side of his face, and then started back up again. This time, smiling triumphantly, Mast did not wait but launched himself down the slope at Grace as soon as Grace was in range, and they went rolling down the slope together, punching and grabbing at each other. This time they rolled more than half way down to the chimney before both intelligently decided to stop fighting until they could get themselves stopped from sliding right on over the edge.

After that, neither of them ever got back up to the trail again. The moment one of them started to try it the other would grab him and haul him back down and start punching him, thus gaining an advantage. After a few of these, neither tried again to get to the trail.

It was a strange, wild, insane fight, there on the steep side of the mountain, with the fluffy pure-white cumulus puffs moving serenely across the deep, startling blue of the Hawaiian sky above them in the sunshine. Far, far below down the steep, incredible skislide of the mountainside the white surf of the sea shone minutely against the black rocks and scattered beaches, and on the highway cars the size of lighter flints moved slowly along, oblivious of the two men who up here still fought.

Mast fought doggedly, tenaciously, slipping and sliding on the steep slope, taking punches that rang through his whole head and body like a great bell, actually heaving and gasping for breath now. It was impossible to kick here on this slope. He could hardly remember what the fight had been about, all he knew was that he had to win it, and that he was being beaten. Grace's arms were too long for him, and while Grace was perhaps not quite as strong as he, Mast knew he was taking three times as many punches as he landed. Even as he continued to fight on, taking one more punch, sliding one more slide, he knew he was defeated. Even though he continued to throw punch after punch, he had resigned himself to defeat. So it came to him as a matter of astonishment and complete surprise when, after a particularly heavy exchange of blows, Grace muttered through swollen lips, "All right. I give up. I'm licked."

Mast, his face swollen grotesquely and his arm cocked to deliver another blow, stared at him through puffy lids unbelievingly. Grace's face was swollen also, perhaps even more so. And the right side of his face where the kick had landed was a liverish purple, and that eye was closed.

"I can't take any more punches on that bad eye," Grace mumbled through puffed lips, not without dignity.

Mast dropped his arm and turned and started off up the slope. Twice he slid to his knees before he got up there and he was not at all sure he was going to make it. But he did, and when he did, he went straight to O'Brien, took his pistol and holster out of his hands, and went to the tent and reattached it to the riflebelt that Grace had taken it from. Then he sat down. As an afterthought he reached for the belt and fastened it around him.

Grace came straggling along a few moments later. He too sat down by the tent doorway numbly.

"And after this you leave my pistol alone," Mast said through puffy lips, staring at him through puffy eyes. "Or I'll give you the same thing again. And if I want to leave my pistol lying in the tent, I will, and you'll leave it alone."

"Okay," Grace said thickly. "But if you hadn't landed that kick, you wouldn't have whipped me. Maybe I'll try you again sometime."

But it was apparently mostly bravado, because during the week more that they remained he did not try again. Mast was glad. Nevertheless, and even though he had stated categorically that he would leave his pistol lying openly in the tent, Mast did not take it off again. It just wasn't worth the chance. He started wearing it in his waist belt buttoned down under his shirt again when he went to bed, and he wore the rifle belt with the clips and holster on the outside. As soon as he was able, which was not until evening on the day of the fight, he informed Grace that he was moving out. He was not bunking with any cheating thief. He took down the tent, unbuttoned his half of it, his shelterhalf, took his rope and his share of the tentpegs, and made himself a bunk with his own shelterhalf and blankets on the other side of the fire.

Anyway, it didn't matter. Above the tent, or about wearing the pistol again. The harmony and accord which had characterized Marconi Pass and the historic first Marconi Pass patrol were shattered. Grace continued to make his bed where the tent had been, sullenly; the other two kept to their own tent quietly. The awareness that they were, after all, still in the Army, and that the Army and their world were in a state of war, came back over all of them. The curious, and almost idyllic, vacation from life as they must live it was somehow over from the moment the fistfight started. When their relief did not show up that day, and then again did not show up the next day, nobody really cared. The day before the fight they would have been overjoyed that the relief did not show up, but now no one wanted to meet anyone else's eyes and there was almost no talking except when absolutely necessary. Needless to say, Mast did not speak to Grace. When, with shouts from below the rock chimney, their relief did show up and began to scramble up onto the slope, they were down to their last half can of water, their last half case of C ration and had already debated sending one man down to see what had happened. No one was unhappy to see the relief, or to be relieved.

Even Mast was not unhappy. As he rolled his pack and collected his gear, the main thought in his mind was that O'Brien had told him over a week ago, about how once they were down he would be after Mast's pistol any way he could. Once as he worked he stood for a moment and looked down the long, long slide to the bottom, where flint-sized cars still crawled along the thread of highway. It was a beautiful sight and just to look at it you would not know that down there lurked men conspiring to take from him his pistol, his chance of being saved. But then, it was a beautiful view from there, looking up here, too. And look what had happened. His serenity long gone, even his memory of happiness destroyed, for the moment, Mast, his face nearly healed by now, prepared to descend again into the maelstrom of Makapoo to do battle for his salvation. At least there, there was Authority. And with Authority, there were rules. At least no one could assault him physically for it. Here, on the mountain, there wasn't even that. Mast, like the rest of them, had become disillusioned with Marconi Pass.

One thing remained, and that was the awareness that they were veterans. It began as they reached the bottom of the rock chimney they had not seen for two weeks and then looked back up, and it increased as they went on down and around the boulders of the runlet to the truck, and it kept on increasing as they rode down in the truck, first out to the highway, then on along it to the CP. They had been the first Marconi Pass patrol, and they had been somewhere and done something these other men had not done.

CHAPTER TEN

Mast did not have long to wait for the next assault against his salvation to take place, once he arrived back at Makapoo. Less than a week, in fact. He had been tricked, lied to and cheated, bribed, and man-handled, in that order. He thought he knew, and had become experienced in, just about every method. But there was one he had never considered: the honest man. In many ways this one was the worst.

But out of it came something else, something good for Mast. And that was confidence: for the first time, real, genuine confidence.

It was now more than three months since the Pearl Harbor attack and Mast's arrival at Makapuu Head with the pistol. During that three months, in which Mast had battled so desperately to keep it, two things had emerged. One was that no one had ever actually assaulted him physically and taken it from him by force; even Grace hadn't done that. And no one had tried to kill him for it. Not that, Mast suspected, someone wouldn't have been willing to try. But the efficiency of Authority precluded that. There was hope to be seen in this, Mast felt.

The second thing which had emerged during the three desperate months was that never yet had anyone gone to higher authority, such as the lieutenant or the two platoon sergeants, about the pistol. Apparently none of these three, neither the lieutenant nor Sergeants Pender and Cowder, knew anything at all about Mast's loose pistol. With all the pistol's changing of hands, the attempted thefts, the jockeyings for position, the angers and rages and fights and near-fights, never did the three position commanders find out about it. With the wisdom of soldiers, or people under the hand of Authority anywhere, all this was carefully kept from them. And not once during all this time had anyone, not even Mast though he had contemplated it, as had some of the others probably, deliberately gone to them and told them about it. That distinction was reserved for Sergeant Paoli, the honest man.

Paoli came up to Mast one afternoon four days after he had returned from Marconi Pass. Short, chunky, dark, a former butcher from Brooklyn, he was a section sergeant in the machine gun platoon under Sergeant Pender and thus wore a pistol himself. Always a 'book soldier' and known laughingly in Mast's company as 'The Book Says' Paoli, he was stupid, unimaginative, mechanically a genius with a machinegun, and short with words.

"I see you got a pistol," he said to Mast, who was working quietly on a detail that was putting up siding on another new hutment. "I seen you walking around here with it long time now, pretty cocky. I know some the stuff that's went on with it."

"Yeah?" said Mast, who did not like Paoli. "So what?"

"It's screwing up the whole position. That's what. It's causing all kinds a trouble and inefficiency round here. That's what."

"Nobody else has noticed any inefficiency that I know of."

"Yeah?" Paoli folded his chunky arms authoritatively. "The book says—"

"I know what the book says, Paoli," Mast said.

"The book says," Paoli said doggedly, nevertheless, "riflemen carry rifles. It don't say they carry pistols. Machine gunners carry pistols."

"Okay, so what?"

Paoli jerked his head backwards, at the command post hole behind him. "I'm taking that pistol. And I'm turning it in to Sergeant Pender."

"You're not taking this pistol anywhere, Paoli," Mast said quite positively. "And neither is anybody else. Nobody's taking this pistol off of me."

"Yes. I am," Paoli said. "And that's an order."

"Order be damned. Nobody's taking this pistol off me except an officer or Sergeant Pender himself.

I've had that stuff pulled on me before."

"You won't obey my order?"

"That order, no."

"The book says—" Paoli began

"To hell with the book!" Mast said fierily.

"The book says," Paoli said anyway, "to refuse to obey a order of a noncom is a court-martial offense." Again he jerked his head backward at the CP hole. "You come with me."

"Sure," Mast said. "Any old time." But the confidence that sounded in his voice was not inside him. Here, now, descending upon him, was the thing he had dreaded most: To be turned in with the pistol: He stood and watched the event shaping itself in time; even though it hadn't happened yet he was already now into the sequence, and it would happen, and nothing could prevent it. It twisted his stomach crampingly. Once again his old friend the Jap major charged down on him screaming, saber high, while he sat and watched him, pistolless. And after all of this, after all of what he had gone through, it would have to be Paoli who would be the agent. He followed Paoli to the hole.

"Tell you something, Mast." Paoli slowed his pace. They threaded their way between two outcroppings. "You got no right to have a pistol. Where you get it?"

"I bought it," Mast said wearily. "From a guy in the 8th Field."

"Well, you got no right to it. And somebody stole it. You're a buyer a stolen equipment. That's bad. And how you think I feel? Me and my boys in my section? We got pistols. We was issued them. But we ain't got rifles. You got a rifle. You was issued it. But you wasn't issued a pistol. Yet you got one. You got a rifle and pistol both." His voice was accusing.

"So has Sergeant Pender," Mast said. "And so has the First Sergeant."

"They're first-three-graders," Paoli said. "You're a private. Everybody knows the pistol's the best defense against them Samurai sabers. Okay. But what about the defense against a rifleman? For that you need a rifle. I ain't got a rifle. Me and my boys in my section. All we got is pistols. But you got a rifle."

"In other words, if you can't have a rifle, I can't have a pistol?" Mast said.

"That's it," Paoli said.

"Why don't you buy yourself a rifle?"

"Where?"

"Anywhere. Look around." But Paoli, having had his say, characteristically did not answer this and clumped on.

They found old Sergeant Pender sitting outside on a rock outcropping scratching himself in the sun. He looked up at Paoli noncommittally as they came up.

"This man refused to obey a direct order, Sergeant," Paoli said without preamble.

"Yeah?" Pender said. "Well. What was the order?"

"I ordered him to give me that pistol. So I could

turn it in to you. He refused, Sergeant."

"Well," Pender said. He scratched his three-day stubble of beard.

"He says he bought it off a guy in the 8th Field," Paoli said stolidly. "So it's stolen equipment. He's a buyer of stolen equipment."

"Looks like that, doesn't it?" Pender said thoughtfully.

"That's a court-martial offense," Paoli said, and Mast looked at him, at his dull, perpetually injured face, at his bulling-head stolidity, that did not know it was injuring Mast, or anybody or anything else in the world for that matter. It merely went bulling ahead. Mast hated him. He stood and thrust hate at him as if it were sacks of cement, or bricks.

"That's right, it is," Sergeant Pender said.

"And he refused to obey a direct order from me," Paoli said. "I want to turn him in to you for that too. The book says—"

"I know what the book says, too, Paoli," Pender said.

"Yes, Sergeant," Paoli said.

"Mast's not in your section, is he?"

"No, Sergeant. He's in a rifle platoon. But he's got a pistol."

"If he's not in your section, why'd you take it on yourself to turn him in, Paoli?"

"Because he's got a pistol. That's what. The book says riflemen supposed to have rifles but not pistols."

"Okay, Paoli," Sergeant Pender said. "Thanks.

I'll take care of it. You can go."

"Yes, Sergeant," Paoli said, and turned on his heel and left, the set of his chunkily muscled back showing how well he thought he had done his duty. Pender stared after him thoughtfully.

"Well, Mast," the old sergeant said, and scratched his stubble again. He made a wry grin and shook his grizzled head. "Looks like I'll have to take that pistol of yours and turn it in to the supply room."

"I suppose so," Mast said, feeling sick at his stomach. He put his hands to his rifle belt to unclasp it. He knew Sergeant Pender fairly well, although he had never run around with him or got drunk with him of course, any more than he had with any of the first-three-graders.

"Look, Sarge," he said suddenly. "Isn't there any way I can keep it? Anything I can do to keep it. It's—it's—important to me."

"Why?" Pender said.

"Well, it's—Well, I bought it, you know? And it—it makes me feel more like a soldier, sort of. You know? And it's a mighty good defense against those Samurai sabers you know."

"Yes, it is that," Pender said in his gentle way. "You mean you sort of feel it's insurance."

"Yes, I guess. Sort of."

"But not everybody has them," Pender said. "You know that. Riflemen don't carry them and machine gunners who have pistols don't carry rifles. Do you want to have a better break than the next man?" He peered at Mast shrewdly, his eyes glinting.

Mast didn't know what to answer, whether to tell him the truth or to lie. If he lied and said he didn't want a better break than the next guy, he would be forced by sheer logic to give up the pistol. And anyway, old Pender would know whether he was lying.

"Well, yes," he said finally. "Yes, I guess I do want a better break than the next man. Let me put it this way," he qualified, "let's say I want every break I can get for myself. Whether the next guy has them or not. But I don't want the next guy *not* to have them."

"Unless it's your pistol," Pender said.

Mast nodded. "Unless it's my pistol."

Pender's eyes glinted again, even more so, and he suddenly grinned, showing his stubby, broken, stained teeth. "Well, I guess that's only human, hunh, Mast?" he said. Mast's answer seemed to have pleased him in some way. For a moment he scratched his grizzled head. "Well, you know, I saw you with that pistol before. And I wondered where you got it. But I figured what I didn't know wouldn't hurt me any. So I didn't see it any more." Pender raised his eyebrows and shrugged ruefully. "But now that it's been brought to my official attention by Paoli, and everybody knows it, I don't see what else I can do but take it and turn it in."

"I don't think much of anybody knows it's been

brought to your official attention, Sarge," Mast said. "Unless Paoli tells them."

"Paoli will tell them," Pender said.

"I suppose so. Then there isn't anything I can do to keep it?"

"I don't see what, Mast. Do you?"

Mast bobbed his head. "You've got one, Sarge. And you've got a rifle, too. The First has both a pistol and a rifle, too."

"I'm supposed to be issued a pistol."

Again Mast bobbed his head at it. "But everybody knows that that one's your own, and that you brought it with you into the company."

Pender looked down at his grimy thigh and slapped the holster on it. "This one? I've had this one since 1918 in the first World War."

"Please let me keep mine," Mast forced himself to say.

Again, Sergeant Pender scratched his grizzled head. "I tell you what, Mast. This is what I'll do. I'll just forget Paoli brought you up here and turned you in with it. How's that? I can't guarantee any more than that. If the lieutenant or somebody tells me I have to take it away from you, why I'll have to do it. But until then, I'll just forget Paoli brought you up here. How's that?"

"That's fine," Mast said, smiling all over. "That's swell." Then his face sobered. "But what about Paoli?"

"I'll handle Paoli. You send him back up here when you go down." Pender paused a moment. "Paoli's a genius with a machine gun," he added apropos of nothing, in an expressionless voice, and looked off at the road. Mast felt it was a partial explanation.

"You know this might really save my life someday, Sarge," he said gratefully. "Thanks. Thanks again."

"Yes, it might," Pender said. "It might do that."

Mast turned to go. "Sarge, how did you come by your pistol? In the last war."

"I stole it off a dead American," Sergeant Pender said expressionlessly.

"Oh," Mast said.

"But his bad luck was my good luck. He did me a big favor. Because it saved me twice," Sergeant Pender smiled. He scratched his beard, and his face sobered slowly. "And I don't *really* believe he had any more use for it. Do you?" he asked.

"No," Mast said, feeling suddenly strange. "How could he?"

"Well, I've wondered about it," Sergeant Pender said. "Sometimes." He coughed. "You send Paoli up."

"I will, Sarge," Mast said eagerly, smiling all over again.

The chunky Paoli did not change expression or say anything beyond an expressionless, clipped "Okay," when Mast came up to him still wearing the pistol and told him Sergeant Pender wanted to see him. And Mast stood and watched him go on off chunkily up the hill. Then he picked up his hammer, but he could not go back to work yet. For one thing his hand was trembling violently, and so were his legs, and the thought of his near-escape made him suddenly go weak all over. He sat down by himself on an outcropping, the hammer dangling from his hand.

Out of this had come the best of all possible things, the best position he had been in since first getting the pistol. He had Sergeant Pender on his side. If the lieutenant, who rarely seemed to notice anything, or some other officer, didn't notice it and made him give it up, he practically had it made. And why would an officer notice it? and if they did, how many of them would give a damn?

There would be other attempts to steal it, undoubtedly. Other bribes, attempting to gain Mast's salvation. Other tricks, other subterfuges. But Mast was sure he could handle all of them. And the thing which all along had troubled him most, since he had bought this pistol from that man in the 8th Field Artillery, the thing he feared the worst: that of being turned in with it: was no longer a problem. Mast felt safer now with his pistol, and with the chance of survival it gave him, the chance of being saved, than he had ever felt since he had had it. What could possibly happen to it now?

And as the weeks passed, he became more and more reinforced in this opinion.

CHAPTER ELEVEN

It was not that there were no further attempts against the pistol during those next several weeks he had it. There were quite a few. But the thing that was different was that the tone, the quality, of everything had changed. It had changed because Mast himself had changed. Something, some word, some phrase, that old Sergeant Pender had said to Mast had in some indefinable way relieved him of some indefinable something. Perhaps it was a guilt about the way he had come by the pistol: buying it like that. Or perhaps it was simply pressure that he was relieved of: the simple pressure of waiting perpetually to be turned in to Authority. In this instance at any rate, Sergeant Pender *was* Authority; and he had upheld Mast. Or perhaps it was merely the knowledge that something like this with the pistol had happened to human beings before, was not a totally unique experience without precedent or guideposts to follow. And not only that, had happened as far back, as long ago, as the first World War, which was already ancient history.

Perhaps it was due to a little bit of all of these things, the change of quality, the change in Mast. Whatever it was, it had given him confidence. It had given him a belief, however erroneous, that the pistol was really his own now. Consequently, he was able to handle the new attempts against the pistol almost easily.

O'Brien was the worst offender during those weeks. One day he slyly tried to exchange belts with Mast when they were in the shower together at Hanauma Bay, but Mast had been too quick for him. Another day O'Brien showed up at the open-trench latrine while Mast was there, obviously hoping to snatch the pistol while Mast was incapacitated, but Mast had been too smart for him there too, and had had his belt with the pistol on it between his squatting feet. And there were other, similar incidents. O'Brien was always around, lurking somewhere in the background, a scavenger waiting to swoop in at the first false step, the first relaxation, and relieve Mast of his salvation.

But if O'Brien was the worst, there were also others. None of the old ones—Winstock, Burton, Grave, even Paoli—really had given up either, and there were new ones whose eyes were greedy. Mast did not care. He could handle all of them. And if he had to live in a constant state of apprehension and tension, that did not matter either. He was more than willing to make that sacrifice for the sake of the pistol.

Old Makapoo had changed considerably during those weeks. The hutments they had worked on so long were completed now, and everybody had a dry place to sleep out of the wind. Another, greater change was caused by the bringing of the regiment up to full strength finally. Replacements, new, green, freshly drafted men from the States, were arriving in hordes and being assigned to regiments and companies which had been under-strength since 1920. As a result there were now almost twice as many men at Makapoo as there had been in the first days, and rumors were already abroad that the regiments of the division were going to be relieved and shipped out, possibly to Attu, possibly somewhere south. There were even books to read now at Makapoo. A traveling library, fitted out with display shelves on both sides of a truck, had been added and was serviced by the Red Cross along with their canteens. It came around once a week. Old Makapoo was becoming almost civilized, and Mast like the other oldtimers at Makapoo never tired of telling the new men, the replacements, how tough it had been in the beginning.

Everything considered, Mast could almost be said to be quite happy, if his constant state of nervous apprehension and jumpiness over the pistol were discounted. And whenever he thought of those rumors about moving out, possibly into combat, he did not mind the nervous apprehension, not at all.

Nothing could get it away from him now, he was sure of that. What possible way was there that he could lose it?

It dawned clear and cold that day, and as always just at dawn and at dusk, the never-ending, unceasing wind across Makapuu Head fell away to a sudden eery silence louder than any noise for perhaps fifteen minutes. Mast had come off post at the machine guns in hole number five at five o'clock, and since it was so near dawn he stayed up to see it. The thin, violet pencil-line of light along the horizon out at sea grew slowly, spreading upward toward the zenith, slowly turning itself red as it grew, tingeing the scattered clouds with red, then orange as it swelled and swelled, an inexorable lightening of the world, irresistible, not to be stopped. Mast always had loved watching the dawn come up when he was on post.

After the spectacle was over, and feeling refreshed as only dawn after a night awake can make one feel, Mast went down to his hutment to get his mess gear for morning chow. He had just spent two hours sitting in the pitch black of a pillbox, staring out intently past the snub barrel of the .30-caliber watercooled at even deeper blackness in which Japanese ships could not be seen had they been there, until his eyes had wanted to cross themselves or lock themselves open. As always the tension of staring, of expecting, had told on him, worn him out as it did all of them, and now he was hungry. But tired or not, hungry or not, he had his pistol to console him. It was a thought which always came to him at such moments, and he rested his hand on it as he stood in the chowline.

He waited half an hour for the kitchen truck, another ten minutes for the line to move back to him, ate ravenously, cleaned his gear, and walked back to the hutment to get the book he was reading. So far it was just another day, a nice one. Work details were getting fewer and fewer at Makapoo and there was more time to loaf and read. He sat down on an outcropping with the book.

O'Brien was sitting not far from him on another outcropping, reading a comic book, which the traveling library thoughtfully provided also. Their association was still the same as it had been since that last day at Marconi Pass, because O'Brien had not given up on the pistol. It was in effect an armed truce. They spoke to each other abruptly and stiffly and that was all.

Now, as Mast sat down, O'Brien looked up from his comic book, his pale green eyes cold and hard, and nodded stiffly. Mast nodded back.

Just another day, like any day.

He had been reading perhaps an hour, and it was just about nine o'clock, when another weapons carrier came roaring down the road and turned in at the position. It was too soon to be the noon chow truck, obviously, and the breakfast one had already gone. -Mast, like everybody else around, looked up to see what it could be. Weapons carriers from the CP were always big occasions. The sentry opened the wire gate for it and it came on in, and then Mast saw that it was Musso who was in it.

Perhaps it was at that moment that he had his first premonition. At any rate, it was then that his heart surged and then began to pound loudly in his throat. As he watched—with a sense of seeing inexorable, inevitable movement which made everything seem to slow down to an unbearable slowness—the little weapons carrier stopped, Musso unwound his long legs out of the seat well and got out, came walking over toward him. He was unbuttoning his shirt pocket as he came. And Mast merely sat and watched him come.

It was all very simple, really nothing at all. It took but a moment to complete. Mast didn't actually *feel* anything, except the pounding of his heart. All that would come later. But at the moment there was really nothing to it. Perhaps the most horrifying thing was that Musso had no idea at all of what he was doing, none at all. He was simply doing a job, and a trivial job at that. He was not angry at Mast, he was not even grinning at how Mast had almost 'put one over,' he was simply picking up a lost pistol.

He was, if Mast had been forced to voice it, assuming Mast was able, which Mast was not, simply and inexorably Authority. The personification of absolute, inexorable, impersonal Authority.

"I've been looking for that damn pistol for over a month," Musso said indifferently. "Couldn't figure out where it disappeared to. I knew I was one short, but I couldn't figure where. Never thought to look up that old peacetime guard issue."

He had already pulled out the old requisition Mast had signed so long ago, so many eons ago that it was even back before the war. It took but a moment for Mast to unhook the pistol and hand it over, another minute to go inside the hutment and bring out the lanyard brassard and web pistol belt.

"Okay, kid; thanks," Musso said and turned and left, other more important jobs obviously on his mind.

Mast was still standing, looking after him. Near him O'Brien had gotten up and was standing too, his face totally blank with disbelief and horror. Slowly he moved closer to Mast, his arms dangling disbelievingly, impotently. Mast hardly noticed him. He was thinking that the worst thing was the question which kept running through his head: Had it all been for nothing? all the worries? all that effort? the fight? all that concentration? really all for nothing. He had actually forgotten somewhere along the line that he had ever really signed a requisition for that pistol. Wasn't that silly? He really had believed he'd bought it.

Down below them Musso climbed back into the carrier, and the sentry opened the gate, and Mast simply stood. As O'Brien was simply standing, beside him. As the weapons carrier crawled out slowly through the gate, O'Brien began biting his lower lip furiously, as if the full import had finally reached him. Tears of rage, or frustration, had come into those pale green eyes of his, and his face was dark with anger.

Then, as the little weapons carrier with Musso in it shot off down the road and began to dwindle into the distance, O'Brien suddenly flung up a big fist and commenced to shake it after the dwindling carrier.

"You got no right!" he shouted. "You got no right! It ain't fair! You got no right to do that to us!"

In the violence of his emotion he threw his head back and yelled it at the top of his lungs, so that in an odd way, while he was shaking his fist after the carrier, O'Brien himself, his teeth bared, was staring fiercely upward at the sky, as he went on shouting.

"It ain't fair!" O'Brien shouted upward. "You got no right! It ain't fair!"

And beside him Mast stood staring at the picture of his Japanese major, who would someday come for him.

Dell Bestsellers

JOSEPH WAMBAUGH

author of *The Choirboys*

THE BLACK MARBLE

Joseph Wambaugh's "best novel yet!"
New York Daily News

Five Months on The New York Times Bestseller List

The Black Marble is Wambaugh's fifth bestseller and first love story! It tells the story of two unforgettable characters: Sgt. Valnikov, a damned good cop who turns far too frequently to the warmth and solace of Russian Vodka, and Natalie Zimmerman, an energetic woman detective determined to preserve the sanity and order of her division and to avoid at all costs the bad luck of the Black Marble. Together they fight crime, boredom, and each other and find more than they had ever hoped for!

A Dell Book $2.50 (10647-8)